LIGHT
the story of a girl

Laura Ross

Staten House

Staten House

Printed in the United States of America

First Printing, 2019

ISBN 979-8-89778-334-2

Follow me around: **IG:** *lmwrites50*

Contents

Prologue

"WHAT HAPPENS WHEN THE sun is out?" Emilio asked me in a low voice.

I looked at him and sighed. "Will you stop pulling that poetic crap with me?"

I really did hate that. Emilio was always doing stuff like that when there were awkward silences and weird moments between us—just like now. We were in homeroom for the first day of school and the class was as loud as ever. Louder than last year. Hell, it seems every year they get louder.

I took a deep breath and found my voice, "Listen, I know you love your poetry, but I'm just sort of stressed out right now, okay?"

He looked at me with a wide grin and challenged, "What a spunky *chica*! That's what I like."

We basically hugged and made up. We hadn't seen each other all summer long, because my family had to go to El Salvador. As it turned out, my great Aunt Suela was dying. So, it sort of ruined our aspect of 'vacation' and changed it to 'drastic visitation'. We were on the phone a lot though- Emilio and I. However, I trusted him the entire time I was away. Emilio wouldn't do something like that to me.

So I thought.

With all spontaneity, this chick walks up to Emilio and whispers something in his ear, looks at me, and walks away.

"What the hell was that?" I shouted. The class was silent. Emilio scratched his head and smiled awkwardly. Without thinking, I pounced on the skank that was halfway toward her seat.

As I was pounding on her, I was grinning when I realized the answer to Emilio's question:

Light touches everything.

Playing with fire

"WHAT'S THAT?" GABBY ASKED me in Spanish when she walked into my room unannounced, eyeing down the eyesore of a poster. It was the beautiful picture of Emilio Ricotti and me hugging each other, but his head was barbarically hacked away from the picture. Emilio and I were always breaking up and making up on a regular basis- I was the usual one to make it clear that we weren't speaking or together. Gabriella Reyes was my mother, and she knew very little English. After all, we moved from Spanish-speaking Florida only three years ago, so she was a little star crossed between a hot dog and a futon. But I loved her anyway.

I learned most of my English through school. I was listening to music on my iPod, and she sort of scared me.

"*¡Dios mío!*" I exclaimed, placing a hand to my heart as I stood and walked over to her. "Ma! Knock next time." I imitated knocking gestures with my hands. "*Knock!*"

I was determined for her to understand English. I ushered Gabby out the door and shut it. She was so annoying! Barging into my room without knocking should be a sin. She was very religious so I knew that would have made her emphasize her entrance. Whatever it was she needed to tell me so badly...never mind. I threw my iPod in my drawer and cut the TV on. There was nothing on but a bunch of paid programming and cooking shows. I wasn't that much into infomercials and frying eggs, so I switched it off. Shying from that, I guess it was all right to mention my twenty-four year old brother who was still mooching off my parents. He had a room down the hall from mine, which he used to sneak *gringas* upstairs. I was the only one who knew about them, he didn't know I knew, but I wasn't going to let him know that. His name is Enrique Reyes; a playful post grad that said he would join the army once he "got on his feet." I didn't believe it until I saw it in writing. Which I still didn't.

I actually knew what Gabriella waltzed in my room for. I think we all could guess why. She didn't trust me after that...incident eighteen months ago. However, I assured her that I was no longer a dumb girl. What happened was the past and I was willing to get over it. I had no idea if my dad, Pablo would get over it. Well, he was stern and alpha male, so I doubted he'd be showing his emotions soon.

Pablo Reyes worked dayshift and night shift in retail. We had a family business sort of thing going on. My dad bought and sold property in El Salvador, but in the U.S., he just brought buildings and turned them into stores. Like tattoo bars, Deli's, convenient stores, and Laundromats. It was a bit more fun to just walk in the store and ask the employees to make you a sandwich on the spot. I know they just put it on my dad's tab though. When Pablo came home the house would always seem to light up. We're laughing and joking or dancing or singing just for kicks. His face lights up when he comes in to see us all there— alive and well.

I got up from bed, threw my shoes on, and combed my shoulder length ringlets out. I sprayed it with some oil sheen and threw my hat on. Next week would be the first week of my junior year in high school. I could not wait to leave school after senior year though, and to me it was the beginning of the end. After school, I'll probably find an apartment somewhere, not here in Queens though. There was no way.

When I walked through the living room to leave, I was feeling for change in my pocket. Yes, there was a twenty in there. I was wearing my mini skirt and was surprised that I found anything in there at all. I rarely put items in that tiny little pocket. I shrugged and exited the house without waking anyone up. I guess I was always a morning person, not many people would enjoy waking up and walking to the store for something. Anything, really.

I went to *Reyes*, our family store, and saw someone I thought I'd never see again. I truly thought he'd run away this time. Ironic that he was in the same store the same time as me. I could feel the hate bubble inside me as I walked toward the minors' section to buy my item.

"What's happening Ray—"

I got what I needed and dashed for the check-out. He followed me.

I handed the cashier the money and then exploded, "Juan, leave me alone!" He was on my trail as I attempted to get away. I stopped and waited for him to walk up to me.

"I just want—"

I swung my loaded shopping bag in his face.

It threw him back for a minute, but gave me just enough time to make it down Elmer Street.

"I just want to see her..." was his voice trailing off from the distance.

Once I made it inside the house, I shut the door and locked it. He knew where I lived of course, and I didn't want to see the bastard. I looked down to see a crying little girl crawl toward me and touch my toes. I sat my bag of pampers down on the floor, and picked her up. She stopped crying when I held her. Her eyes were glistening and she was pouting.

"You're ugly when you cry Jasmine."

She smiled, not understanding a word I was saying. I guess I never got around to mentioning that I was a mom.

I never said my name

REINA REYES WAS ME. Jasmine Reyes was my daughter. Was I forgetting anyone? I guess I have to explain, huh? I can't just say, "Hi, how are you, I have a baby." That would be kind of weird. Well, Juan Cruz is my child's father, obviously. And one night at a party, things just happened. That's all I could say. In the beginning we were cool...real cool. Hell, he was actually one of my best guy friends. Oh yeah, he didn't attend high school anymore. He graduated five years ago, in fact, he was one of my brother's friends initially. They don't talk anymore since what happened with him and me. It was sort of a shame, really. He was twenty now and I had heard rumors that he had gotten out of college- to visit, I mean. I guess it was true then.

"Did you have breakfast, *mija?*" She was babbling so I took her in the kitchen to make her some cereal. It was that nasty baby rice cereal- all organic crap. Gabby thought it would help her bones, but I thought it gave her the runs. Well, a mother knows best right? So I guess that was why I allowed Gabby to help raise her.

"Bray bray!" Jasmine was yelping and being her normal happy self, it was obvious she hadn't eaten for quite some time.

"All right, all right. You're fed, now where would granny be? She was supposed to feed you." I was cooing to her in my arms, while searching for my mom. I was calling her and calling her, but there was no answer. The house was silent, and that was really rare for my house. Enrique was always bringing some of his loud ass friends over and trashing the upstairs. I climbed the stairs to see that no one was...home. How could that be? My father was hard at work, Gabby should be here, and Enrique...I wasn't surprised when I noticed his disappearance.

As I roamed the halls I wondered, since I had the house alone, to myself, I figured something. We owned three vehicles: the *Jeep*, *Toyota*, and the *Explorer*. The *Jeep* was never there because my father worked day and night. I just got my permit a month ago, so I went with my gut.

I nearly fell, when I strode down the steps. Shoot, I basically galloped toward the garage. The *Toyota* was gone? Where the hell was she? Gabriella didn't have a job, nor could she speak good English. The farthest place she could go without me or my brother was the backyard. I felt a slight twinge of concern, but was still bubbling with excitement to get out of the house again. Once Jasmine was strapped inside the *Explorer*, I hopped in and took off.

I parked in front of Emilio's, and waited. He would be out soon; he was seriously paranoid so that's how I knew that. I never liked going in his house. It was always full of gangbangers and weed was always in the air. Emilio wanted me to meet his mother, a kindred spirited Italian woman with good morals. She went to church every week and always remembered to brush her teeth; she was that sort of lady. I was surprised as to how she could live in a house full of delinquents every day. I guess she had some tolerance.

As always, Emilio showed up at the door, smiled, and jogged toward me. I unlocked the passenger seat door, and he got in. "How are you?" He asked me, looking at me in a funny way. *Gawking* at me. I nodded, it meant I was fine. He turned to look at the back seat, I rolled my eyes, and he chuckled, "I see you brought the little one. She's gotten big."

"The last time you saw her—oh, yeah. She got to know her mother's roots in El Salvador this summer." I looked at her and saw that she was sound asleep. That explained the silence. I started the engine, and pulled off. I was making a left when, I turned to him and asked, "Are we...over?" I said this with a small voice. Three months ago, before I left for El Salvdor, we had a huge fight over something I didn't remember and now I was going to start school *boyfriendless*.

Emilio looked at me and said, "We'll get to that later...you're going too fast. You should slow down." I glanced at the speedometer and slowed the car to a decent speed. I pulled in to the pancake house and turned the car off. We were sitting there in the quiet for exactly five minutes. Yeah, I know it was pathetic to count right? "Emilio..."

"I'll get Jasmine— unless you want to..." he continued, "I'll see you inside."

He got out of the car, walked around it, and pulled at the handle. There was a knock at the back window, I turned and heard him say in a muffled voice, "Unlock the door! I can't get to her." I released the back locks and he opened the door to grab my daughter from her car seat. I watched him walk into the building with her resting at his shoulder. She was still a little drowsy from her nap. I sighed and eventually got out and joined them inside.

I had been feeding Jasmine when Emilio inquired, "Do you think I would've been..." He was watching me and her sadly. I wondered what was on his mind. "Reina...I want to tell you something."

"What?" I asked casually, no use in getting my hopes high or anything. It was pointless now, he never answered my question. "Is it bad?"

"Reina, the love we share was all I had.

You cheated on me and made me sad.

Though I never wanted to come off as mean.

Even if the infidelity resulted in Jasmine. I'm sorry..."

So he just *had* to get poetic on me and bring *that* up.

A small chat over coffee

I DON'T KNOW IF I was even comfortable thinking of that night. The night I...got with Juan Cruz. He was always the epitome of our problems and fights- what happened eighteen months ago. Juan and Emilio used to be friends, and Juan always had a crush on me. Crazy, right? Juan, Emilio, and Enrique were like really tight in the past. I try not to blame myself for their split. I was so drunk that night. All I can recall was conception and the following morning. Well...that's not the whole truth, I do remember a little more than that:

"Reina, you have got to come to this party!" Luz exclaimed in my ear.

Apparently, she had some friends that had some friends that knew these people who got her into the club. Emilio and I were going steady then, we were somewhat "lucky in love". I never thought that Emilio would actually admit something like that though.

"Luz, hold on, what are you talking about? Slow down!" She sounded excited, way too happy, maybe even drunk. I was shaking my head when I remembered who I was talking to; Luz was all the way out there.

The music was making her scream into the phone, "Reina! Get out of that house girl, this party is hot!"

"Luz, I got homework—" I started to complain, but she interjected, "Milio's here."

Just in case you're confused, that was Emilio. I was cheesing at the thought of seeing him...partying. Drinking, moving with the music. I was all excited when I answered, "Well...what should I wear?"

Luz screamed into the phone, "Go *au naturel*, girl! Wear it out!" I looked into the phone with a questioning frown. I chuckled and corrected her, "I said 'what should I wear'- as in clothes."

"Girl, I can't hear you— I'll call you back." And then there was the dial tone. I shrugged and placed the phone back on its base. I was now rummaging through my closet, hunting for a halter and some jeans to wear. I just had to look good for Emilio. I really did love him-still do. It was just that night...when everything went wrong. When I was finally dressed, I crept downstairs and noticed a figure on the couch. "Oh, sh..." I whispered, but the voice beckoned me. "Poppy...is that you?"

"Yes, it is. Come here, Reina."

"Si." I agreed sadly, I really wanted to go to that party.

When I approached the figure on the couch, I sighed in relief and punched him.

"Ricky! Stop playing with me!" I couldn't deny the relief that was flowing through me. "Don't tell Gabby and Poppy that I'm leaving."

I dragged in a long breath and headed out the door. I wasn't all that legal to drive, and I wouldn't be able to since I knew I would be intoxicated by the end of night. I didn't exactly plan how I'd get home as I should've, but I knew pretty much anyone at that party would offer me a ride home.

My eyes were fluttering and for a moment I had to recover from the sudden burst of emotion that was dominating my conscience. Emilio finished his pancakes and asked, "Is Jasmine still having that digestive problem?" I had to come down to the ground to answer the question.

Numbly, all that came out was, "Uh...um...n-no she's fine. Really, why?"

Dumb question. Emilio was constantly worrying over Jasmine's health. A little more than he should...especially with him not being her father...

"That poem- the one you just recited- I thought we were over that. That was like eighteen months ago... I thought..." He just chuckled with dark humor. Frankly, I had a short temper. "Never mind."

"There's nothing wrong...I can't...I don't know how to tell you this. So..." His eyes glazed over for a moment, when he finally spouted in rapid Italian, "*You are the sweetest person I'll ever know.*" And here we go again, I thought. I dreaded whatever his next words would be, yet anticipated them at the same time. And then the desire to cry dominated the anger. Maybe this was for the better...

Emilio stood then, and said, "Um, *accidenti,* I'm gonna' take off. Take ca-"

"You can't just up and go! You can't leave me, I don't understand what you said to me just now, but I don't like it." I was standing and his eyes were bulging with sorrow. "Reina, sit down, you're making a scene!" He whispered mostly out of fear that I would be embarrassing myself, I knew him that way...he was selfless...perfect...too good for me. I could bare the whispers and incredulous stares coming from the audience, but not the pained expression of the man before me. Jasmine began shouting, and I wanted to pull my hair out, and the whispers grew louder, and- "Be quiet!" Emilio shouted. Everyone in the pancake house obeyed as did I. "Reina! Are you deaf or just plain stupid, I am...I love you girl, can't you see that? You always make something out of nothing, now just..." Jasmine's cries grew strident and more frantic. Emilio took a breath closed his eyes and choked out, "Take her home, tuck her in, and...I'll see you later. "

"Emilio, what about-"

He was outside by then, walking down the road we traveled to get here.

"What is wrong with you?" Gabby asked in brisk Spanish when she saw me storm through the house angrily. When I finally stopped to acknowledge her question, it was too late- well past lying- before I knew it, the tears were pouring down my face. Making me look like a sobbing pup. A hopeless one, too. She cradled me in her arms, how could I explain that? There was nothing like a mother's touch... seriously, when I lay in her arms I felt so protected against the world's worst enemies.

But I could never tell her that.

After all, I was a mom myself, how would I seem wanting *my* mommy? Immature; that was Jasmine's job.

I looked down into my mother's eyes, really because she was so much shorter than me, and cleared my own. "Nothing's wrong mom..." She didn't know English that well, but she could tell I was lying. She was skeptic, "You lie. You lie. Tell me- was it Juan?" Of all times I could've denied that question, shrugged it off, or just plain ignored it- there was no escaping the ugly truth. That major something that would follow me around, possibly, for the remainder of my existence.

It was my fault.

Following no specific pattern

I HAD TO REMEMBER to breathe. Inhale, exhale, and to continuously switch. The next four days passed by numbly, lacking any real purpose. Emilio was absent from school those four days, I tried to call him, but it sent me straight to voicemail. I was also trying his house phone, which was rarely on, and Ms. Ricotti answered to remind me of his absence. I couldn't bear hearing the rumors of what happened to him:

He ran away and eloped with a hooker.

He got locked up for assaulting a teacher.

He killed a man.

He moved back to Sicily...

Just hearing his name brought back that day...seems like yesterday when he told that he didn't want me anymore...sounds needy...but that about sums it up. I had been spending the next few days trying to get out of bed. Emilio was gone. He was the little bit of sanity I had. How would I live without that single piece of sanity?

"Hey, um, Reina can I ask you a question?" I ignored whoever it was and kept my head down; they knew I wasn't up for it- talking. Why would I be when everyone knew that Emilio Ricotti and I broke up? I sighed and rolled my eyes. I would not control my reaction if whoever that was tried to ask me a question again. After about ten minutes, the bell rang and the entire class basically ran out the door. I lagged behind this day; this was the worst mistake I would have ever made. "Reina, right?" I exhaled sharply and snapped, "You've asked me two questions, leave me alone!" I didn't appreciate how people made me explode like that; I was trying to better myself...not the other way around. "My bad...I was just wondering if you were free Friday night. Are you?" It took so much in me not punch him in the face. When I turned around, we were in the hallway by my locker, yes he followed me. Whoever this was, he needed to quit his day job. I shucked in a breath, and said mechanically, "What do you want from me?" He hovered over me with gentle features, and a nice face. He was black, with dreads, and owned a certain charm that I could not stay angry with. "I go by Ross Nolan, and I think you should know that I'm no good at this."

All right so I guess I had to press him. "At what?"

"You know, uh, speaking to beautiful ladies." *Beautiful lady? Me?* Whoa! Now I was certain of these three things:

He was not from here.

He was most likely gay.

Whatever he was on, it really must be some strong stuff.

"Oh!" I exclaimed halfheartedly. This realization made my head ache. "You're the new guy from Philly! Am I right, or was I just dreaming in class again?" He gave way to a throaty chortle. "Yeah, that's me." It took him a while to recover from my discovery. I stared him down for a long while, just until I got a feel of who he was. That's it! All the girls were after his ass, especially the boyfriend-less, and I didn't know if it was because he was new, or genuinely his looks. He wasn't a bad-looking kid; if I wasn't so deep in shit, then maybe I would've been one of the many who lusted after him.

Too bad I wasn't interested.

"All right, all right. It seems I shouldn't persist on this-well, see you later Queen." I rolled my eyes and nodded, then flinched on that last part. "What!" I yelped. He was strolling down the hall when he called, "Your name, that's what it means...and that's what you are." And a few minutes after he left, and the bell rang, I reached a conclusion:

Yep, Ross was high as hell.

Dancing over the horizon

As I descended the stairs I noticed my mother freaking out on whoever was on the phone. She had been yelling all sorts of profanities in Spanish, and that alone let me know who she was talking to:

Juan Cruz.

I knew that he was the only one in America that could drive my mother to her boiling point. I stood there and listened to the conversation—well, on my mother's end for that matter—and winced. I couldn't help but think of what ever made me sleep with that asshole. I mean, jeez!

Just as I went to give him a piece of my mind, Gabby slammed the phone back on the base. Whispering all the painful things he'd endure if he were in person.

When she saw me she sighed and said coldly, "That was Juan. He said he wanted to visit Jasmine." She snorted. "Like I would ever let that happen."

"Mama..." I said in warning. "That isn't right; you know that—remember what the judge said?" Of course she remembered; she was the one who decided we'd get it done. Yeah, he really wasn't her favorite person in the world.

She looked at me warily, "Of course *bebé*, I remember. Every other weekend he is allowed...uh...visitation." She said in her broken English. I was so proud of her. "But..." She looked down.

"But...?" I said, urging her on. She looked up then and said to me. "He wants meet with you to...um..." She finished the rest in Spanish. "He said he wants to take Jasmine with him to visit his family..."

I rolled my eyes. Was that what she was fussing over? Last I heard, his family lived in Brooklyn. "So, what's the problem?"

She hesitated. "His family is in North Carolina."

"Open the got-damn door Juan!" He gave my mom the address to where he was staying while he was in town; surly enough I took it and ran. How could he do something like this?

The door opened to reveal a half-naked Juan Cruz, wearing nothing but a white sheet around his waist. Any other day I would have laughed my ass off, but these were under different circumstances. This involved my child.

He yawned and made a face, "What the hell Ray?" I knew he intended for it to sound a little more coldly, but his fatigue made him sound harmless. I was so through with this; first he isn't around for most of my child's life, and now he decides to take her away from me? Uh-uh, no way was I having that. Giving me an appreciative once-over, he said lowly, "So I guess you heard about me wanting to take Jasmine to the south, huh?" I had to inhale and exhale very slowly to keep my calm.

"What the *hell* do you think?" I said through my teeth. I swore I was seeing red when I finished, "Why are you doing this to me?"

He gave me a droll stare and said in a bored tone, "Why so selfish *miel*? I'm not doing this to you." He sighed and pinched the bridge of his nose. "My family just wants to see her. Show her a good time, ya know, so she can get to know the other side of her roots. Is that a crime? I mean, you took her all the way out of the country."

Man, he was such an ass! It was hard enough trying to reason with the guy, now he was just being plain impossible. I opened my mouth to speak when he moved aside. "Why don't you come on in, *miel?*" He offered, using the Spanish term for *honey*.

"No! And will you stop calling me that for Christ sake?" Making this an all-time sigh-a-thon, he rolled his eyes and stepped out onto the little porch—standing not two inches from my chest. He shut the door behind him and smiled, looking between the little space that stood between us. Automatically, I stepped back and glared at him. "Stay away from me; I'm not here for that."

He chuckled. "Oh? And just what are you here for *miel?*" Swallowing the distance, he took a step toward me; grinning that familiar grin that got me in so much trouble in the first place. I shook my head as if to clear it; when I spoke the sound was muffled in the hollow of his chest. Angrily, I took a step back, putting a good foot between us. There. "To discuss the welfare of my daughter!" I screeched.

He winced then growled, "She my daughter, too, dammit! And it's not fair!" I widened my eyes in disbelief. If a bat suddenly materialized from nowhere—I'd have a few good uses for it. "What's not *fair* Juan? That you're an asshole regarding Jasmine, or that you're pissed because you're stuck with us?" I shook my head, my glare was calculating. "I bet you're ashamed of her."

Juan had a tic in his jaw when he averted his glare to the ground.

"Why, you fucking lowlife, you finally admitted it huh?" I scoffed. "I knew all along that you were ashamed of her."

"That's not what I meant! Ray—"

"That's enough, Juan, you made your point!" I said gravely. "Your family's gonna' be really disappointed, cuz there's no way I'm sending her there now." I sniffled. Damn, I was betrayed by tears. Shaking my head, I turned and started for my truck. As I started the engine, I saw Juan just standing there in his sheet, frowning at my car. It took so much in me not roll the window down and flip him off, but I managed by grabbing the wheel and speeding back to Queens.

***

"Where you been, *chica?*" Ricky asked me when I stomped in the house. I just glared at him. He gave me a knowing smile. "I see I just signed my death certificate. Damn, what he do now?" I knew he meant Emilio, and I had no idea why I had this sudden urge to correct him.

I sniffed, "No, I'm talking bout your boy Juan." I inhaled sharply. "Such an ass."

Now that caught his attention. His expression turned solid. I actually didn't know if it was hate or confusion. "Cruz back in town?" He frowned and asked lowly. "Where he stayin' at? You know?" Oh shit. My brother was a playful guy and I never had to worry about him getting angry. But the expression on his face looked like he wanted blood.

"He stayin' with his cousin Rico—wait a minute, why you want to know?" He shrugged like it was no big thing.

"No reason." Enrique was part of a gang, the Latin Crips, or LC's, and they were serious business. The reason I knew about it? Well, a few years back, he ran through the house panting and finally he came to my room. It was nighttime, and he woke me up and told me he needed a place to hide his gun. I told him he could hide it in my room as long as I knew where and why he got it. Said he got it from a friend and that he needed it for protection from whatever rival gang was after them. And it's been in my room ever since. He stood up and, stretched, and started for the door. "I'll be right back."

"Nah, where you goin' Ricky? Tell me!" I swallowed audibly. Shit, when he was in this mood, it scared the shit out of me. He stopped and turned around, frowning like nobody's business.

"Yo, you cryin' Ray? Hold on, I'll be right back." I started to protest, but he already slammed the door. Well, damn, I just couldn't win today.

The rest of the weekend passed by, mentally, without me in it. So when Monday morning came, the alarm rang and scared the hell out of me. Apparently, I wasn't the only one, because when I turned around I saw Jasmine freaking out in her crib. I sighed and stood to attend to her. "There, there," I whispered and picked her up. She was one heavy nine-month old. At the sound of my voice, she quieted down and I laid her back down in her crib.

Thankful for her not fussing again, I crept to my closet and threw on pretty much anything. My black leggings with my cut-off jean mini skirt pulled over it, and my long sleeved , fitting black shirt. I decided to wear my hair down this day, so I scurried on to the bathroom, dug out my flat irons, and began experimenting with the tangles. After the flat job, I announced that I was leaving, grabbed my backpack, and started for the horn outside. When I opened the door, I spotted Luz Lopez, a dear friend of mine since the ninth grade, waving at me from her black *Range Rover*. To the untrained eye, she looked like any other black girl. But when she spoke, those ideas were squashed. Her skin was lightly tanned and had full dark curls that hung just past her shoulders and a big smile. Her family wasn't rich, but upper-middle classed. Her father was a dentist, Dr. Lopez, and her mother was a nationwide businesswoman. So, her being an only child had its benefits, financially. "Come on girl, time to go! School time!" She sang.

When I got in the car, she hugged me and then started the engine. I laughed and said, "Well, hello to you to."

She guffawed. "Woo! Had a *great* time this weekend! Went to the baseball game with Joey—" she wiggled her fingers—"and got my nails done!" Oh yeah. Luz had the potential to work for any major law firm, medical practice or something along those lines. She had good thinking skills and was smart as shit. I'm not saying that her need to become a beautician was asinine or anything, but to me, a person with that kind of potential would be financially and spiritually upward bound.

And she was as fickle as a damn bird. Every two weeks or so she had a new, "boy toy". I actually thought it funny, her inability to commit, but her family didn't like that. Apparently, each guy she brought home her parents didn't approve, and they would find that *one* thing they didn't like and use it against Luz. After her rant, Luz turned to me with a deer-caught-in-the-headlights sort of look. "Oh, I'm doing it again. My bad. So what have you been up to girl?" She knew what I had been up to this weekend, so I didn't bother to answer. Hell, everyone knew what was going on between me and my missing boyfriend. I swallowed, held my chin high, and glared at her. She just licked her lips awkwardly- a habit of hers- and made a left on Elmer Street. Once we reached the place I hated most, we got out and started forward with the crowds of teens heading inside the building.

Luz was nervously babbling on our way to our first period, which was usual, but today things seemed strange. It was as if she was talking to avert my eyes from peoples' stares and whispers. I sighed and finally asked loudly, "What is going on here?" She hesitated so I added, "Am I, like, the main attraction or something?"

I could hear her gulp before she replied, "Pretty much." I nodded. It was always like that. Whenever something happened in this school, Queens Heights High, it was like a plague. Spreading crap that eventually makes someone sick. Yeah, a shame I know.

When we reached our seats, which were naturally side-by-side, someone finally cracked. "So what's the deal with Milio? He dead or what?" Robyn Newton, one of the Queens Heights's cheerleaders and bitches. She was one of those girls who kept her ebony skin nice and oily, and her hair long and flat ironed. She had the biggest eyes I'd ever seen anyone have, and her outfits usually ranged from skimpy to slutty.

My teeth grinded against each other; I really couldn't stand that whore. She was all the things I just couldn't tolerate: Whiny, trashy, instigative...

Emilio's ex- girlfriend.

I sighed. It just wasn't getting any easier for me lately. "No, Robyn. He isn't dead, sweetheart. Okay?" Luz interjected in a preschool teacher's voice. Speaking to Robyn like she was an idiot—which she was anyway. Ha, everyone knew she was easily intimidated. Point for us.

LOL, she flipped Luz off.

"Not on your life, honey!" She called after her.

I threw my head back and laughed.

The beauty of twilight

"Is this seat reserved, *pour moi?*" A deep voice asked from behind me. I asked Luz to give me a ride to the library when school ended. So I could catch up on the work I didn't understand in my classes. Obviously, I was having some trouble with my French assignments lately...okay, I've always had trouble with French, but still.

As it so happened, I recognized that baritone way too easily. I sighed; this Ross kid was seriously becoming annoying. I could understand if he had a thing for Latinas, but in this case he'd have to search elsewhere. I had as many guy problems as I could deal with.

Scratching his dreads, Ross took a seat beside me and flashed a cheesy grin that revealed polished teeth. It was actually kind of charming. I decided to ignore the hell out him—which turned out to be as irritating as him speaking. Otherwise, he just stared at me while I attempted to study. My temper getting the best of me, I snapped, "Will you quit gawking at me?" I began frowning at my homework. I knew the guy only, what, two days and he had already become a pest.

Ross looked genuinely offended. "I was *gazing*, not *gawking*, there's a huge difference. Gawking is staring dumbly and fixatedly at something. I was gazing—truly appreciating my focal point, Queen." The last part of what he said struck like a bat to the head. "Don't call me that, Ross."

"I didn't call you 'Ross', I called you by your name." He said stubbornly. That was when I turned to him and lost the battle against the smile that was tugging at the sides of my mouth. "Childish much?"

He playfully scoffed, "Only when I gotta be."

I nodded. "So, would you kindly grace me with the reason of this visit?" I asked a little less coarsely. Ross shifted slightly in his seat as if uncomfortable by the question. I watched him as he considered what to say to me. "Well, I came to see if you needed a little assistance. You looked a little tormented over here all alone."

I gave him a hard stare that showed I hadn't believed him.

"Okay, I came here with some friends to study, and a few minutes later you walk in. Now as I'm sitting there thinking a realization hit me: why not meet you over and compare notes? So here I am, trying yet failing to ask you out to lunch." His expression meant it as a question. I opened my mouth to deny him, but thought instead. Why the hell not? It wasn't as if I had anything else to do—besides French. But I'll just finish up at home later. It's not like I was agreeing to an orgy or anything, just lunch. A good time. He stood and said in a low voice, "Look, I should have never come over here...so I'mma let you get back to your studying. Later, Queen."

"Ross wait," He halted in his tracks, and looked over his shoulder. I could see the hope in his eyes as I said, "I'm in." He laughed and smiled that goofy smile that was growing on me and exclaimed, "Woohoo! Let's go girl!"

Druggies and finger-paints

WE WENT TO THE little café, The Stream, on West Avenue that was just around the corner from the park. Ironically enough, as much as I passed by here, I never noticed that hidden novelty that was, "Just Around the RiverBend".

Carrying my backpack, Ross opened the heavy seeming doors with ease, and allowed me to enter first. Yikes, the first smell that hit me was a strong dose of vanilla. I mean seriously, I could handle a gentle hint of it, but it *reeked* like *Bryers* gone wrong. Looking around at the customers, I saw that no one seemed to notice it; they actually seemed to like it. For me, however, it felt as if my lungs were getting clouded. "Manager's sort of a larkspur freak—sorry." Ross whispered. Aside from the smell though, everything inside looked new, expensive, dim and homey all at the same time. There was a woman onstage reciting poetry with a baggy, beige hat and dressed in a tan, but professional, one piece. She also wore her hair in dreads as Ross did, and chocolate-colored flats. The look would have looked homely on anyone else, but she managed to pull it off, especially with the passion and eloquence as to which she spoke. Her voice was melodic and it demanded attention in the large room (which seated about a hundred people by the way).

"Shall we be seated, Queen?" Ross asked with laughter in his voice.

"My name is Reina." I blurted on impulse, never taking my attention away from the woman on the stage. As we sat at one of the small round tables in the middle of the room the poet finished with a booming, "And you will NOT break me!" And with that, there were lots of snapping going on. I turned to Ross, confused. He was snapping, too. When the noise died down, he whispered, "You're not supposed to clap at a slam."

"Why not?" I asked.

He shrugged. "I guess it's just classier not to do so." He nodded toward the stage where a good looking black man was now on stage announcing in his rich deep voice, "Everybody give it up for Spyrit Abiola Faith!" —More snapping—"Now as you know, today is Monday, which is Free Slam day. Now I hate to take it back to the old school, but let me see some hands for whoever wants to go up next." Several hands flew up, and a devilish thought occurred to me. I turned my attention to Ross. "Raise your hand, Ross. Go ahead." He looked at me as if I told him to walk to Brazil, which was a *bitch please* look. I took that as a challenge and raised my hand, out of all the people in the joint, the host's eyes immediately went to me. "Yes! A young soul has decided to recite. Come on up girlie."

I shook my head. "No thank you, but I wanted my friend here to go up there." I pointed to Ross. "He's a little shy." The spotlight shone directly on Ross. He had a weary look on his face but stood up anyway and headed over to the mic. The host smiled and handed him the microphone, "Thanks Dad." Ross greeted the host as he walked offstage. My eyes widened, I knew he was related to him! They looked just alike, except in the dreads department. Soft music began to play, and Ross took control:

"Things change—you all know that

I can tell you all now, I know all about that

I knew this girl once who broke my heart

And pain's a part of change

She told me she loved me and I her

Things were getting serious, too

And there was this bench we went to all the time

We chilled there

But you all know, things change

Till one day I decided to take a walk

To clear my mind

And lucky me, I caught her in the arms of another

Did I flip? Oh, HELL YEAH! (Ross shouted, and I jumped. Yikes, never seen that before)

Just on the inside though

On the outside, I stayed cool when I asked her why

And do y'all know what she said? No?

Take a guess...that's right...THINGS CHANGE!"

With that final shout, the crowd began to snap furiously. Ross was panting, and he looked grim, no dangerous. Feral almost. Whoever that girl was must've hurt him bad to evoke that side from him. He smiled after he composed himself and turned to walk off the stage.

"Did you order anything while I was up?" Ross asked when he finally made his way back to our table. I frowned, confounded only for a moment until I realized that he meant food. "Yeah, I hope you like clam chowder and hot cocoa." Ross sat, picked up his spoon, scooped some up, and globbed it back in his bowl. He shuddered. "Here I thought you absolutely loved clam chowder." I said teasingly. Whoa, I should stop that. I didn't want to lead him on. He sighed, shrugged, and reached for his cocoa. "Nah, it's cool. Thanks for the cocoa though—it looks as if it's about to rain anyway." And with that, he slid his chowder over to me and chuckled. "You have this one, I'm good boo." I swallowed the warm, yummy stuff that made me happy inside, and shrugged. "Hey, more for me." I took his bowl and poured its contents in mine. Mmm...

"You should probably get going though, it's getting late." I turned to the window, lightning lit the sky and rain was coming down in buckets. When I turned back to him, I lifted my brows as if to silently say, *you don't really expect me to walk in that, do you?* He answered with a nod, laughter, and standing up. "Come on, I'll drive you home. You can take a to-go platter if you want or whatever. Don't want you hungry girl." He smiled kindly, and we walked over to the counter where a woman who looked to be about in her mid thirties was wiping down the kitchen area. Her long hair was in a ponytail and she wore a brown t-shirt with the logo, The Stream, on it with white ink. She was smiling warmly at Ross and me. Suddenly I felt guilty to ask her for any kitchenware; it looked as if she were cleaning up for the night. "Oh, I don't want you to go to all that trouble, I'll just—"

"What? Throw it out?" She shook her head. "Now that would be insulting; here, I'll wrap it for you." She took the plate and poured my chowder into the plastic bowl and handed it back to me. I smiled and thanked her. We began to walk away, when her voice stopped us. "Ross, where are you going boy?" The kitchen lady asked in a chiding tone. Jeez, who was she his mom? Ross answered to her sheepishly, and held up his keys, "I'm driving her home, Mom. I'll be straight back, I promise."

She nodded her approval and went back to her business, wiping the counters. My eyes bugged when I realized how and why that was his mother. We were in the black car, which was a new edition Navigator by the way, when I asked, "Is that a family business or something?" Ross just turned left at a light, when he asked, "Where do you live, Queen?"

"Elmer Street."

"Gotcha," He sighed and turned another corner. "Okay, so you could call it a family business I guess. But this is my Dad's second shop. He has another one, ran by one of my Aunts, in Philly. I moved here to help out in the new shop. I Wait there after school every afternoon. Today was my day off." He started slowly down the long strip of houses on Elmer Street. "Which is yours?" I looked out my window and saw a tall figure on the porch, waiting up for me I guessed.

Ugh, Enrique. "The one with the pissed off Mexican on the porch." Ross nodded in understanding and parked in front my house. In a flash, Enrique was walking toward the car, ignoring the rain. He glared straight passed me, at Ross. "This car is nice enough to sell for parts, *hombre!*"

"Stop it, Ricky! Go back in the house; I'll see you in a minute. I need to thank my friend."

"But Ray—" I held my hand up to silence him, he hushed instantly. "I'll be there." I said finally. With a grunt, he backed away from the window and stalked back inside the house. He left the front door wide open; the bastard was trying to advertise my late arrival. What was his deal? I sighed when Ross said, "It's all right girl. You good, just give me a hug and get on out of here. I've got curfew, too." I smiled, leaned over and gave him a friendly hug. Apparently, he didn't think so as I pulled back and he caught my lips with his and kissed me. It was a nice...well, more than nice kiss that had me breathless when it ended. Stunned, I clumsily scrambled out of the car, stuttered my thanks, and climbed the porch step. I could still feel the tingle of the kiss when I walked in the house to find a beaten and bloody Emilio Ricotti on my living room sofa, dying.

Bathing in ice cubes

"IS REINA HERE YET?" Emilio croaked. I gulped down a lump of bile and opened my mouth to speak. Instead of forming words, I dashed over to him and my words were broken sobs when I said, "Yeah, baby I'm here. Why aren't you in the hospital?" His face was swollen and beaten blue and purple and different shades I couldn't stand to describe.

"It's gang related. He can't go there, or they'll notify the authorities and he'll be gone for good. It'd be his third strike, Reina." Enrique was speaking for him, and making me angrier.

"Ricky you're annoying the hell out of me! Just-Just tell me what happened here?" Yes, I was aware that Emilio had been in jail before, and was out on probation. I also knew he was LC, like my brother, so I know this pissed him off more than anything.

"He was staying with Kenny for a while, and he sent Milio to the store to get him some liquor." Ricky started. "While he was there, some Bloods saw him and jumped him. When he got here, he passed out."

Yes, Emilio was only eighteen, but the LC's had connections, so I didn't press him any further. "I tried calling you, but you left your phone here. I was gonna go look for you, but Milio asked me to wait here for you to come back home. I had to anyway; I didn't want him to bleed to death on the couch, or to leave the baby alone." I was shaking uncontrollably when I heard a hard thump, Enrique punch his fist through the wall. I turned to him and asked, "Does Mommy and Poppy know?"

He shook his head. "They're not here, Mommy called and said they'd both be late handling business and shit." His voice trembled. I noticed he was fighting tears. "Can you believe those bastards had the nerve to hang around *Reyes?*" I recognized the name of my father's store instantly, and realized that's how Emilio got here so fast. Our house was just down the street from the store. Thunder clashed angrily outside, scaring the hell out of me and making me think of my daughter. "Where is Yaz?" My voice was clipped with emptiness, as I kept looking at my boyfriend fading in and out of consciousness. His eyes closed and I shook him—gently—so he wasn't asleep. "Uh-uh, wake up Milio." I turned to Ricky. "Make sure he stays awake, okay?"

He nodded, wiped his face, and mumbled, "She's asleep in your room. I fed her already." I thanked him and trudged upstairs. Could my day get any worse? That question was confirmed when I opened the door to a screaming infant. I sighed and hurried to her crib. As usual, when I picked her up, she stopped crying and tried to sleep again against my shoulder. As I rocked her, I wondered what to do with Emilio. Where was he going to go? He couldn't go anywhere tonight, he was way too wounded. When my parents came home, what would I tell them. "Oh, hey guys. What's that over there? Oh, it's only Emilio, he's dying you know?" When Jasmine was fully asleep, I laid her back down, took my shoes off, and went back downstairs. Not even bothering to get undressed. I felt too guilty to get comfortable knowing Emilio was on the couch in a thousand times more pain. But me, I was broken emotionally, and I knew from here on out, that things would never be the same again.

***

Thankfully, our parents hadn't come home all night. Where the hell were they lately? It seemed they were never home anymore. I wanted to stay up and watch Emilio all night, but Enrique insisted I sleep upstairs and watch over Jasmine. I agreed, and in the morning found Enrique in the chair, asleep sitting up, and patrolling over Emilio's body. I shook my brother gently, and he woke up letting out a stream of swear words in Spanish. I held my hands up in surrender, "Wake up, it's time to get Emilio home." I walked over to the kitchen counter and took the keys to the *Explorer* and tossed it to him. Sleepily, he stood, stretched, and trudged over to Emilio. He shook him, lightly, and his eyes slowly fluttered open. I sighed in relief, thankful he wasn't in a coma. Actually, the swelling to his face went down...sort of. But he did look better. Rested. He didn't look tired and beaten up at least.

It was seven a.m., and I had already dressed for school; I called Luz last night and she already agreed to take me to Selma's, my babysitter, house the next morning. After Jasmine was dressed and bundled up for the cold, I eventually grabbed my baby bag, cell phone for sure, and daughter and headed out to the blaring car horns outside. Luz was here. I left Enrique money for gas, just in case, and got in the car to a silent Luz. "Selma lives on Charles Street." I told her once I got Jasmine safely in her car seat. She revved the engine and started down the street, we rode in silence the entire drive.

Once Jasmine was dropped off, we noiselessly rode to school, no radio blaring or Luz's usual zeal. When she parked, we got out and, you guessed it, walked silently inside the building. When we reached first period, I sighed and finally said, "Luz, what's up girl?" She looked at me, doubt in her eyes, and uttered, "Nothing, I'm fine."

"Hey baby!" An exuberant voice came from behind us, I sighed, man was he annoying. Joseph Corazon stood at a whopping six-foot three, towering over us. He was an avid soccer player and had an innocent appeal to him I just couldn't explain. He was also Luz's boyfriend. From behind, he hung an arm loosely around Luz's shoulders. She cringed and shrugged them off. What the hell was going on? Usually, they were all over each other. "Hey Joey." She said uneasily, looking around as if she was guilty of something.

Her discomfort hadn't fazed Joey a bit. "You coming to the game tonight?"

Luz forced a smile and nodded slowly, not meeting his eyes. "Yeah."

He smiled and ducked to place a kiss on her cheek. "That's why I love you baby." He turned to me, nodded, and left. I had begun to ask Luz what her deal was when the bell rang for first period to begin. Luz hurried in and I barged after her.

We took our usual seats in U.S. History at the back of the class. There were juniors pouring in, so I took advantage of the noise to ask, "Are you okay?"

"I'm fine!" She snapped. Several eyes lingered over to us, but I shooed them away with my hand and slid my desk closer to her. I leaned in closer to her and said, "Luz...spill." She sighed, and that's when I knew I won. "I-I did it..." She whispered. I sat there confused, and blurted before I could think, "Did what?"

Her eyes were filling with tears when she locked gazes with me. That's when I knew what she meant. Not even caring about the people watching us, I reached over and hugged my best friend. God knows that I knew how she felt. Since Mr. Smith wasn't in class yet, I grabbed her hand and pulled her toward the door.

"Where are we going, Ray?" She asked when I stopped abruptly and held my hand out to her. My answer was instant, "Keys."

She was reluctant to take the keys out of her pocket; well that's what she looked like. I sighed, gave her a quick hug, and continued to lug her outside.

When we reached her car, I unlocked the doors and got inside the driver's seat. Normally, Luz would never allow anyone in this seat. Damn, she was some kind of depressed to allow me entrance to this side of the car.

When Luz and I were safely buckled in, I started the engine (which ran like butter) and took speedily off. It was actually then when I understood where I should be, stupid though it may sound, I knew the next place to park this car; and that place was the stream.

The pursuit of grief

"SMELLS LIKE VANILLA IN here...real bad." Luz noted as we walked inside the little café, wincing slightly. I couldn't blame her though, the aroma still made me a little woozy. Looking around though, I noticed there were less people here than the first time I came, and instead of there being a poetry reading, there was only a low melody playing in the background. I grabbed her hand and lead her to a small round table near the window. "They have the best clam chowder here!" I told her excitedly. She smiled warmly. That was a relief; I'd rather her like that than sullen like before...which reminded me...

Time to face the music. I smiled sympathetically at her, "You wanna talk about it?"

Her eyes widened, then realization passed through her eyes and she looked about guilty. "Not much to tell. It was quick and painful all right?" I could tell from her tone that she was growing a little indignant from the subject. We sat in silence, and from out of blue came a question that was *loaded* with meaning. "So," Luz began slowly. "What's been going on with you lately?" I looked down, and considered my response. Should I tell her all of it? I mean, I knew I could trust her, but could I trust myself? Sighing, I looked my friend squarely in the eyes, sighed, and answered, "Well, guy problems mostly; consisting of Juan wanting to take my nine month old out of state, Ross the New Guy slowly yet surely seducing me, oh and he kissed me also. Emilio, broken and bloody, was on my couch in the middle of the night jumped by a rival gang of his and my brother's. Oh and speaking of Ricky, he'll probably go after whoever did it and possibly get him and whoever else killed. And my parents are never home so now I have to keep my time clocked, and constantly pay a babysitter who I don't think is all that right in the head." I drew a deep breath. "Other than that, I've had a pretty good week so far, you?"

She opened her mouth to comment, but was interrupted by a stronger voice. "Sounds like you got some demons there, girl!" A woman with shoulder length dreads put in, walking up from behind me. I had begun to tell the broad to mind her damn business, until I got a good look at her when she halted in front of me. I gasped. "It's you—uh, Spyrit right?" Huh. I didn't know why I got so worked up, but I did. No point in going back now. She smiled slyly, and extended her hand to me. "It's nice to meet one of my fans." Her eyes slid over to Luz. "Hello to you, too."

Luz looked nervous, "Uh, hi."

Spyrit nodded once, and said, "I see you know me, but how is it you know my favorite nephew?"

"Nephew? Who?" Luz blurted, sounding like her old self.

Spyrit ignored her interjection and looked directly at me. "I heard you say you were starting to like him."

I looked away. That was none of her business. I had enough issues as it was without— "Well, I didn't mean to pry. I'm just visiting the family from Philly and helping out over here. So, what would you like to order?" A pen and pad was in her hands instantly. I looked at Luz, she smiled politely. "How about some of that famous clam chowder Reina keeps yapping about?" She watched me pointedly. I shrugged and mumbled petulantly, "I love clam chowder."

Spyrit laughed good-naturedly, wrote something down on a piece of paper, and slid it over to me.

There was a number on it.

Before leaving, she whispered, "Just give it a chance." Standing straight she wandered off while muttering something about us supposed to be in school.

"You're right, that chowder *was* good!" Luz said in hurried excite. About two hours passed since we'd ditched school, and so far Luz and I were having a good old time. We talked about all kinds of stuff; like the time I first moved to New York three years ago from El Slvador. We were cracking on Luz's ex-boyfriends and how lame they were now. Why the weather was so weird and if we believed in the story of 2012 or not. "It's ridiculous," Luz said between bites of chowder. "People have been saying that the world was going to end since before we've been born. I'm still here, so why should I be shaking in my boots now?" I rolled my eyes and smiled. There was never a way to truly tell what would happen in the future, was what I wanted to say, and that if the world did end that I would at least want to go in peace. I should have said something, but decided against it; the topic was too depressing. Glancing up from my super sized bowl of food, I caught a flash of pain in her eyes. Concerned, I extended my hand over the table and placed it on hers and squeezed gently. She looked up, and I didn't even know how we got to that topic, but her voice was trembling when she said, "Joey...he said that he loved me, Ray." Tears were streaming down her face. She sniffled and continued, "I don't know what to do."

"Oh, Luz," I said, my voice pain-stricken. I didn't like to see my friends hurt. Hell, I didn't even like to see anyone hurt—no matter how much I despised Juan, I didn't wish him any pain. Not like this.

She shook her head and continued, "I don't know Ray. How do I know he's not lying to me? If-If he's just not saying things because of...last night." At the mention of that, her eyes watered more and she put her face in her hands, totally weeping. I stood and hurried over to her side of the table. Kneeling, I wrapped my arms around her torso and we cried together. We didn't say anything for a time, but after a while, I was back in my seat. We were both wiping our face. I took a deep breath for strength, knowing I'll need it, and said, "You'll never really know. You just have to give it time, and if both of you can still stand each other than that's how you know you're at least getting somewhere." I thought my voice was strong and sure, but instead it came out as a small whisper. It was all too painful to think of Juan now. How he lied to me, used me, and then cast me aside and moved on with his life. If only I hadn't gotten pregnant, I'd bet money he'd be in college somewhere far away from New York—long gone. I had been such a fool back then, how could I have been so stupid? For as long as I knew Juan Cruz he always had a crush on me. He, Emilio who I was currently dating back then, and Enrique hung out all the time. I would often tease them of their "bromance," but they denied it and went back to playing video games or whatever.

It wasn't until Rico's party that Juan acted on that "crush."

Okay, so it wasn't rape or anything, he was actually very gentle despite the drunkenness. I was drunk, too, and my vision was clouded. It wasn't that I thought he was someone else, I knew it was him. It was the reality of it; I didn't think it was actually happening. And the fact that it did, the fact that I allowed it, tore me to shreds. In one fell swoop, I had lost everything: my virginity, my boyfriend, my self-respect...

"You okay?" Luz's question and concern brought me back to earth. I didn't realize she'd been talking while I was lost in my thoughts. I sighed, thinking of it that way made me feel like a bad friend. I looked up from my chowder and reassured her, "Yeah, um, could you say that again?"

Luz rolled her eyes before she continued, "*As I was saying,* even though I'm sort of mad at Joey, this is a big game. So, are you going tonight?" Queens Heights were up against Mascaw High—and rumor had been that they played to assassinate. Well, our soccer team was good too, but it took some serious training to go up against Mascaw. It was too bad I couldn't go though. "I'm sorry Luz, but—"

"Oh, come on Ray! After all we've been through, you can't just do this one small thing for me?" I thought I heard anger behind the beseeching. Huh. I guess I heard wrong. "And there's nothing else I'd like to do, but you know I can't. I would have to pay Selma double." To myself I muttered, "The old witch." Plus, there was no way I was going to just leave Emilio that way. After school, I planned to go over to Kenny's, who was one of Enrique's best friends, so I could check on him. Just to see if he was still breathing in the least. But there was no way I was telling Luz that much truth. I gulped and began to toy with my chowder. It was cold now. "Your parents can't watch her? Or Ricky?" Her eyes were hopeful.

I shook my head. "My parents have been gone for, like, ever." I wasn't going to mention Enrique, he was handling gang business. And I didn't like to interlope on those grounds. I mean, I was a tough *chica* when I needed to be, but gangbanging was rough shit.

Luz nodded in understanding, and stood. She had one hand on her hip, and the other extended out to me. "Keys." She insisted. Nodding, I dug around in my pockets and found the metal key chain. When I handed it to her, she asked, obviously irritated, "You want a ride home or not?" I shook my head. Elmer Street was just a few blocks from here; even Selma's house was close to this place. Luz shrugged, mumbled a half hearted, "Later," and was gone. I heard the engine rev, and watched her gun it back down West Avenue, leaving me alone.

The importance of light

I WAS ABOUT HALFWAY home, until I heard a calm voice from behind me. "Hey miel, over here!" There was only one person I knew who dared called me that. When I turned around, I noticed his sleek *Lamborghini,* which was custom painted dark blue with black flames on the doors. Yeah, his family was another one doting families who bought their only son whatever he wanted. I scoffed; it was only a wonder why he never missed a child support payment. I didn't slow down, didn't falter. If anything I sped up. Juan drove slowly to match my pace. "Oh, come on Ray! You can't still be mad at me from two days ago! Let it go." When I didn't answer right away he said, exasperated, "Fine. Then let me give you a lift—where are you headed, *miel?"* I considered taking off into a sprint, but I didn't want to egg him on to follow me all the way to Kenny's house. When

I spoke, my words were clipped and emotionless, "I'm going home."

"Well, let me take you there. Come on, get in."

Suddenly, I stopped. When I turned to look at him, I glared at those pretty brown eyes. Rolling mine, I pointed across the street. "Juan, I'm already home." His smile faded when he turned and realized it too. I sighed and continued to cross the street and climb the porch. I felt for my key in my pocket, and just as I began to turn the knob, I felt a strong hand grip my arm. I gasped from the pain it caused me, when Juan turned me around and pinned me against the unopened door. "You bastard, I'll—" My breath caught when I saw the sadness in his eyes. What the hell was going on? When I calmed down, he loosened his grip on me, I watched in suspicion. He looked as if he was searching for the right words to say. When he looked up at me, I could see his eyes watering. Panting, he rasped, "I. Just. Want. To. See. My. Daughter." He enunciated each word as if I knew no English.

I narrowed my eyes, "Juan, I can't—"

He held his hand up to cut me off. "Please...I haven't seen her in two months...can I just...please?" Angrily, he wiped a tear from his face, and sniffled. Wow, in all the years I'd known Juan, he was only arrogant or playful. Charming even, but never that...depressed. It was then when he made me realize how terrible of a person I'd become, how terrible a mother too. In all these nine months, all I'd done was shun Juan, extremely so when it came to Jasmine. And ever since we came back from El Salvador this summer, I hadn't given him a chance to see how grown up she'd become. Jeez, I ought to be smote.

Juan stood in front of me, never meeting my eyes, but still sad. "I've been trying to figure out all this time why you hate me so much." He finally gave way to a sob. "Damn, I just want to see my daughter, Ray—is that a crime? I leave in four days; can't you let me see her just once?" I had this huge ass piece of bile lodge in my throat; I forced it down and nodded. "Yes. I was just going to get Yazzy's stroller so I could walk there." I swallowed my pride and I added, "Would you like to walk me to Selma's?" There was no back seat to his car, so that was his only option. He cleared his throat, stuck his chest out and agreed, "All right."

"How's daddy's favorite girl?" Juan cooed to Jasmine when we arrived at Selma's. She giggled delightedly. I smiled at the reunion, and reached in my pocket to pay what I owed her for watching Jasmine. While balancing his daughter, Juan reached in his pockets and handed the old lady a twenty. She smiled and said tiredly, "May God bless you, child. Y'all have a good day now." Thanking her again, we started back down the street to my

house. I was rolling an empty stroller, because Juan refused to put her down. "I wish you'd told me before that you would be holding her. I would have never brought this along." I said teasingly.

He had been cooing with Jasmine all along. He took the diaper bag from his shoulder and placed it gently on the stroller seat. He turned to me and smiled. "See, the stroller wasn't *totally* useless now was it?" Jasmine squealed excitedly from the sound of his voice. Juan tickled her belly and said, "I know you like being held by dada. Don't worry; mommy's just a little uptight." I slapped him playfully on his arm, grinning. He turned his head and winked at me. I shook my head when a surprising thought occurred to me: me, Reina Jasmine Reyes, was bonding with Juan Cruz

We didn't make it far before I saw and recognized the white *Explorer* pull up in the driveway from down the street at my house. I knew that could only be one person and my parents were away with the *Toyota,*

Enrique, my brother who hadn't seen Juan since the day he found out Juan got me in trouble. Which was eighteen months ago...

Juan grew tense, I could feel it, and apparently so could Jasmine; because the moment Juan stopped smiling she threw her head back and began to cry. "Oh, no *miel*, it's all right." Her cries grew louder which made me want to cry along with her. My heart was pounding so loud in my chest when I saw Enrique frown in confusion at the sight of Juan, Jasmine, and me walking toward the porch together. The instant he saw Juan his features grew stoic, then he ignored him and looked at me. "Take her in the house Ray." He said loudly, trying to speak over Jasmine's cries. Juan's face was pale when he said, "I'll take her if—"

"I was speaking to my *sister*." Enrique turned back to me, glared, and started up the stairs and inside the house. I extended my hands to take Jasmine, still screaming. Juan reluctantly handed her over, placed a kiss on my daughter's forehead, and said goodbye to me before he drove off.

At the sight of her father leaving, Jasmine seemed to scream louder in protest. I rocked her and hurried inside, rushing to my room. When I laid her down she finally quieted. Relieved, I turned to go make her a bottle, and yelped when I saw Enrique standing silently at the doorway, his eyes focused on the floor. His face was tired, as if he hadn't slept in days. My heart ached for him; I had been so wrapped up in myself to not notice my brother's health deteriorating. It seemed it was everyone's goal to call to attention how shitty a person I was. "I was going to walk over there since I'm home early from school today, is Emilio better?"

His face was grim. "Yeah, he's starting to keep his food down. He won't really say anything, though. When he does speak though, all he does is ask for you." I nodded eagerly, unaware of the hot tears that were sliding down my face. I started for the door, but he blocked me. I punched him in the chest in anger. "Move Ricky! He needs me, he's hurting and I want to go to him." He just shook his head sadly and covered his face with his hands. His entire body was shaking when he sobbed, "They killed Kenny, Ray." My heart stopped at the words. Fully crying now, I wrapped my arms around my brother and we just cried together for a long time. Kenny was my big brother's support system. I met him only a handful of times, and even then he was very polite, too cordial for a drug dealer in fact. I just know that through it all he had been there even before Emilio and Juan came into our lives. Enrique spent most of his nights there when he didn't come home at all, and my parents knew what Kenny did, but loved him anyway. I just couldn't believe he was gone...really gone...

Once my brother got a hold of himself, he began, "Somebody broke in and slit his throat. He bled to death on his living room floor. It was a good thing I didn't take Milio there last night. It would've been both of them..." I nodded through my tears. The poor guy. Then something came to me, if Emilio was staying with Kenny, then...?

"Ricky, where's Milio now?" I asked, my voice quivering.

He cleared his throat and ran a hand through his hair. "I took him to his Mom's house. She knows about the gang stuff, so when I explained it to her, she said she wouldn't call the cops. She's taking care of him now."

I opened my mouth to speak but he said quickly, "Don't go there, Ray. I don't want you to see him like that—it's gonna mess you up. Plus, I don't want you going places; it's not safe out there. So after school I want you to come straight home, you hear me?" His face was dead serious. I nodded; when he looked like that it scared me.

He turned to leave and called while walking down the stairs, "I'll make the baby a bottle for you, Ray. I want you to study for that French test on Thursday." I sighed. Of course he knew about that stuff, the nosy rat. It was a good thing, too. I almost forgot that there was no school tomorrow due to a teacher's workday. Boy was I thankful, Jasmine had a doctor's appointment that day, too. There was no way I could handle school now. I walked over to where my backpack normally sat in the corner, and saw that it wasn't there. Where the hell was it? Surely I didn't leave it in my locker, I never used it. Now stressed, I went over to sit at my desk and pulled a sheet of paper from the drawer. I found a pen and did something I thought I never would have the patience or drive to do: pouring my heart out, I sat there and concentrated on the impossible.

I began to write a poem.

Playing chess on the interstate

I WOKE UP GASPING; mostly from the realization that I just missed my daughter's doctor's appointment. My hair was mussed and my clothes were so baggy they were falling off me. Disoriented by the mess, I tripped and fell before I could reach Jasmine's crib. Struggling to stand, did so, and was panicked to find no little girl in her crib. Instead I found that her bed was neatly made, and there was a note on the pink, cotton blanket. I picked it up, heart pounding wildly, and read it aloud for some reason:

Reina,

I knew you would be tired, so I took the baby to her appointment for you. We'll be back late.

-Mom

I released a sigh of relief and trudged downstairs. There was a rustling downstairs, like paper moving around, and the microwave running, and the TV playing the *That's So Raven* theme song. Oh yeah, Ricky had a Disney Channel fetish. It was unnatural. When I made my way into the kitchen, I saw that Enrique had a piece of toast in his mouth, and was adjusting his tie to one of my Father's suits. His hair was gelled back and he had a light mustache on his upper lip that added a professional appeal to him. He looked up at me and smiled gently, as if he was going away forever. I looked around nervously and finally said, "What's going on?" He rushed into the living room and grabbed his suitcase while nibbling on the toast. "I've got an interview today. Didn't I tell you, or was it Mommy?" He shrugged and moved to turn the TV off. Before he did though, he gave it one last long stare. When he met my confused gaze, he said sheepishly, "What? I watch Raven when I need to calm down. Lord knows I needed it too..." I nodded in understanding. There was a lot of stuff going on lately. His lips turned up slightly, "Plus, Raven's sexy as hell. She's a little on the thick side, but I like a woman with extra curves." Enrique did his little; "sexy dance" and I cringed. "Uh, eew! Will you stop dancing like that?"

To my surprise, he laughed.

Okay, was my big brother high on something? He was in the gangbanging world, so I wouldn't put it passed him to be stoned right now. Immediately, he stopped dancing and looked down guiltily. Now that threw me off. His voice was low when he spoke, "What happened yesterday...it really opened my eyes you know? It made me realize that life is too short to be...you know, doing what I'm doing. I don't know, this may sound strange, but I think that Kenny would want me to do this for myself." He paused and his eyes were glassy. "Hell, I hope I get the job!" I shook my head and hugged him with all my might. How I loved this guy. When we parted he composed himself, kissed my forehead, and with his suitcase in his hand he walked out. For a second it was real

ly quiet, then Enrique popped his head back inside the door and said hurriedly, "Lunch is in the microwave, Ray!"

"Thanks." I called after him, but he shut the door already. *Now* the house was eerily silent, as I walked into the kitchen and read the clock on the wall. One-thirty. Damn, I slept forever. I must've been in a coma or something. I just had so much on my plate right now. Honestly, I was amazed I woke up at all; given all this stress I was grateful not to stroke out in my sleep.

When I opened the microwave door, I saw a TV dinner inside complete with a chicken breast, macaroni and cheese, and a brownie. My mouth watered from the sight of it, so I snatched it out and yelped from the heat of it, and cursed as it dropped to the floor. Crying out in fury, I kicked it, stomped upstairs to my room and slammed the door. Not even bothering to clean it up.

I stood and began to pace. What to do, what to do? I wasn't allowed to go anywhere, Ricky made sure of that. And he was dealing with enough right now without me adding to his endless list of problems.

I ground my teeth together; it was all I could do not to scream out from the unfairness of it all. I don't know why I did it, but I sat at my desk and began to write. After the first stanza, I began to relax. I didn't know why, but doing...this helped me think easier. It was actually sort of ironic; I had always teased Emilio for his poetry, or just got plain annoyed with it. But now I had a new-found understanding as to why he wrote it—to simply escape for a little while. I looked around my desktop and saw that there were piles of poetry all over it. *My* poetry. I grinned goofily to myself, filled with pride and continued on in my poem. Each word happened to be writing itself on the paper. Still smiling, I stopped and shook my hands; they ached from three pages worth of words.

After I worked the last cramp from my hand I suddenly realized where I needed to be. Right then, I didn't care what Enrique warned me, rules were meant to be broken. I stretched from that long hour of just writing, and entered my closet. Since it was still sort of chilly outside, I chose my black skinny jeans, black *Nikes*, white fitting shirt, and gray flight jacket. It was cloudy outside, so I chose wisely. I put on my hooped earrings, some lip gloss, and pull my hair into a ponytail. There. I was ready now. I grabbed my iPod, jetted down the stairs, and started my journey to Emilio's Mom's house.

I'd been jamming to the song, "Stick With You", by the Pussycat Dolls over and over and found myself crying from the trueness of the lyrics. Emilio and I had been through so much, and it was only right that I come here. *"Nobody's gonna love me better; I must stick with you forever. Nobody's gonna take me higher; I must stick with you..."* I was singing to the song when I stopped in front of Ms. Ricotti's porch, scared as hell. Gulping down bile, I held my chin high and marched to the front door. I never liked traveling to this side of the neighborhood; well, not alone. Especially this house. There were always so many guys (drug dealers) on Ms. Ricotti's front porch; she treated them all with as much adoration as she did her son.

Tucking away my iPod, I cleared my throat and knocked gently on the door. Ms. Ricotti had radar as to who was on her porch at all times, so I had no doubt she was aware of my presence.

Within seconds, the door was opened to reveal a sad looking, short Italian woman. She coughed once before saying, "Hey, Reina. How are you today?"

I nodded. I was afraid if I said something it would come out as a sob. I ground my teeth together so hard I felt a headache coming on. She sniffled and offered, "You here to visit Emilio?"

Again, I nodded. She waved me inside and started down the hall, into the living room. The interior of the house consisted of wild designs of different kinds of flowers. The floor was a hard oak and solid. Bounce an elephant and he'll return to you, I promise, the floor will be unscathed. The walls were solid, too, there was no way anyone could punch a hole through it. I smelled something tangy from the kitchen and wondered if it was one of her famous Italian dishes. Wanting to take my mind off of things, I asked, "So whatcha cookin Ms. Ricotti?" I inhaled again, yep, definitely something foreign.

"Barbecued Chicken, dear." Oh. I could have sworn it was something else. "I made the sauce myself, so it's an *off* barbecue."

I smiled; she was always resourceful that way. So was Emilio...

She led me upstairs and around a lot of corners until she stopped in front of this truly massive, heavy looking, door. It looked like one of those medieval...warrior throne rooms or something. I was a little excited, and anxious to see my boyfriend...until she opened the door.

Emilio lay there, on this massive bed, eyes swollen shut. I understood now what my brother meant by telling me not to come here. He looked...dead. Or at least like he was dying, as he lay there pale and feeble, I finally caved. My sobs were so loud it woke Emilio with a start. "Reina!" He rasped hoarsely. It sounded as if he was parched. Trembling, I walked toward his outstretched arms, picked up his water glass, and helped him drink. He began shaking his head when I made the glass touch his lips. "He barely eats or sleeps." His mother said lowly from the doorway. "When I cook for him, he doesn't want it. That water has been sitting there since this morning. All he does is sleep and call your name over and over. I began to call you, but I see you made it here on your own." Ms Ricotti had to nearly shout over how loudly I was crying. I nodded, sat the water down, and collapsed in his extended arms. He groaned from the impact. Just behind me, I heard the door shut and knew Ms. Ricotti had left. Wiping my eyes, I sobbed, "Emilio, are you okay?"

His swollen lids semi-opened and he rasped, "Now that you're here, I am." I wanted blood for whoever did this to him right then and there. The bastards would pay when--

My anger subsided when he reached his warm hands out to clear away my tears. Bringing my hand up to his busted lips he kissed my knuckles and whispered, "Don't cry, *dolce...*" I bit my lip so hard I tasted blood, but it was all I could do to not scream. I shook my head and whispered, "You've got to eat for me okay, baby?"

He nodded. "I love you, Ray." He croaked then his eyes closed sluggishly, and then he started snoring. Sighing, I leaned in and kissed his forehead. "It's gonna be all right. I love you too, baby..."

I left the Ricotti household crying a river; I could actually feel my eyes swelling. I scoffed; I knew I looked like shit. I also knew how red my nose looked from the biting winds. Sneezing repeatedly, I hurried home and made my way toward the best part of the house today—the liquor cabinet. My father forbade us from even looking at alcohol, and I knew he would notice it gone when he came home from work, but I didn't care. The moment called for it and so did I. I needed something to numb the pain, and, unfortunately, this was it. Well, let the flames begin.

***

"You are *not* the Father, Robert!" The tall white lady screamed at, well obviously, Robert. I was on the couch in the living room watching *The Maury Show*, and on my second bottle of tequila. About an hour had passed since I last saw Emilio, and from what I experienced today was enough to break me. So, I thought this a good idea instead. Taking another swig at my liquor, I shouted, "That kid doesn't even look like you!" in a slur to the man on the TV. A loud, mannish, belch escaped me the second I finished that exclamation. "Whoa! Excuse me." I said to no one in particular, giggling. I guess you could call it me giving up on life, because a sane girl would be upstairs studying for that French test tomorrow. A sane girl would be watching the *Lifetime* channel in her jammies or curl up with a good book. A normal teenager would have accepted that offer from her best friend to attend a high school football game. And the shame was, I was never that sane girl, or normal teenager. My normality slipped away the moment I found out my parents was to become grandparents. The instant I accepted that beer at Rico's party. The second my boyfriend looked at me with disgust for a time after the truth was out.

The reality of things hit me hard, and from then on I went from giggling and carefree to despondent and weeping. I cleared my throat, turned the TV off, and finished the bottle before my conscience could warn me otherwise and the knock on the door scared the hell out of me. I sighed, stood, stretched, and gave one last burp as I wobbled to the door to find a smiling Ross Nolan on my front porch.

Sun tanning in Alaska

"YOU FORGOT THIS THE other day at the café." Looking concerned now, he extended my backpack out to me. Huh. So that's where my French notes had been all along. I squinted my eyes and held out my hand to receive it from one of the Ross's that stood before me. He looked really worried now when he said, "Queen, are you...*crying?*"

This was where I opened my mouth to laugh, but belched loudly instead. Wrinkling his nose he leaned closer as if to smell me and said, "Ugh. And you're drunk?"

I giggled. "There'sssss two of you..." I wobbled a little and suddenly I was in his strong arms. He cradled me all the way to the long sofa and laid me down.

"No, no. It's okay, don't cry."

I frowned at that, confused until I felt the tears streaming down my face. I was sobbing when he stuttered, "Um, uh, it's okay, Queen. W-want me to, uh, make you something to eat?" I didn't answer, just turned my face into the pillow on the chair.

My voice was muffled when I said. "I just want the pain to go away. I'm just so tired, Ross...so tired..." He nodded, his face pain stricken, and picked me up again. Wordlessly, he carried me slowly through the hall, looking inside each room in search of mine, I guessed. When we reached the shadowed haven, he laid me on the bed. He adjusted it so that I was under the covers. I hadn't noticed how cold it was either; I was trembling. My sobs quieted down, and the last thing I remembered was Ross saying, "It's okay now, I'm gonna make the pain go away...it's okay, Queen." And then there was darkness.

When I opened my eyes I smelled something that my stomach automatically reacted to; oh yeah, clam chowder. I turned around to see the bowl of soup on my desk and scratched my head in confusion. What happened? Was my mother home? Silently pondering, I fully sat up and squinted my eyes at the six foot four handsomeness coming through the door. It was Ross with a blue mug in his hands—a steaming mug in his hands. His smile was bright and contagious; I couldn't help the one that was spreading across my face. "Jeez, you slept, like, what? Ten minutes? I know you can't be sober that quickly!" He walked to the side of my bed and sat down next to me. Mmm, he was warm. And the smell of chocolate hit me hard. I licked my lips in anticipation; I hadn't eaten all day. Then I was reminded of the food on the floor, and the bottles downstairs, and the pounding headache I had. He answered as if reading my thoughts. "I cleaned up downstairs while you were sleep. I didn't want to wake you, but damn, you must have been some sort of crazy when you ruined that Hungry Man down there." He shook his head, and handed the delicious chocolate heaven over to me—I drank it without hesitation. The warmness felt good for my headache. When I handed him the cup back, he sat it down near my chowder, picked that up, and began to feed me. The normal Reina Reyes would have pulled back and slapped him; but as I already established, I had no normality left in me. I felt drained and empty, but what Ross was doing, caring for me at my worst, almost made me feel not that bad any more. Almost.

Actually, the feeding may have sounded childish, but it was kind of...sensual. Erotic. And as I licked a drop of chowder broth from my lips, I found it almost impossible not to purr in satisfaction when Ross sent a way too tempting gaze my way. I tried to think of something else when he placed the bowl back on the dresser, but failed. While he leaned over me, I took him by the collar of his shirt and planted a kiss on his lips. God, it was heaven! I nearly trembled from how good he tasted, and found myself rubbing up against him. And then, too quickly, he pulled back from me and cursed at himself. I was panting, and started to reach for him again when he shook his head. "No. I'm not like that. You're drunk, and I don't want to take advantage of you...or hurt you." He shut his eyes real tight as if he fought with himself over something. I gulped and realized the trueness of his words. I glanced at the pink crib that was a little ways from my bed and felt like shit. I looked down, and realized I had nothing on except a t-shirt. I covered my arms over my chest- feeling exposed suddenly. "So, you hate me because I didn't tell you about my daughter? I'm sorry, I wasn't trying to trick you or anything, I don't think like that. You know what—"

"No. I knew about that." He sighed and scooted closer to me. It took so much not to pounce on him right then, he just looked so freaking beautiful! "I like you for being you, not from what I heard about you. I just don't want to do this with you while your judgment is clouded. I want you *sober*..."

"I *am* sober...and I know what I'm doing." There was a momentary doubt in his eyes. I pulled him against me at once, and finally he didn't fight me or push me away.

And on that chilly afternoon, I, Reina Reyes, made passionate love to the guy I only met while I was in French class a few days ago.

Transpire

Let this be known

That you are not as bright

That was transpired

Though you're no candle

We could all see the liar

Walking on Mars and inhaling mercury

1 MONTH LATER

I WOKE UP TO the smell of warm apples and cinnamon coming from downstairs. I stood, stretched, and started toward the steps. Man was I eager to get downstairs to help my mother in the kitchen. It was mid October and still cold as hell outside, same as forever. It was also the Saturday morning before my brother's, Enrique, birthday on Sunday. Yep, he was an October baby, which explained his usual trickery. My brother was a playful guy, and had a kind heart though, so it was only natural that I genuinely celebrate his special day.

When I descended the stairs I smiled at the sight. My Mother, Gabriella, who had been sewing together a bunch of pink, frilly, pieces of material on the living room couch. Alongside her was my Father, Pablo, who had been watching a football game with a can of beer in his hand—shouting and cursing each time a player missed a catch.

My mother looked up and smiled at the sight of me, "*Hola*, baby! Look at this mess!"

I giggled as she threw a few pieces of cloth in the air above her, exaggerating. I shook my head; her English had gotten way better since last month. Hell, everything had gotten better since last month.

"Hey baby girl!" My Father exclaimed, never peeling his eyes from the game.

I laughed at that, too. When he made that concentrated face of his, I couldn't help but smile.

"Reina?" My Mom asked, distracted by the seam she was focusing on.

I stepped closer, "Yeah?"

She cleared her throat and gestured toward the upstairs. "Could you go get, Yazzy? I want to see how she looks in this Halloween dress I made for her."

I happily agreed and hurried upstairs, a little anxious to see how my ten month old daughter would look in it as well. Laughing, to myself I went down the hall and opened the door to her room.

Yes, *her* room.

Ever since Enrique got that high paying landscaping job in New York City, he moved out and left his old room for Jasmine to use. I sometimes found myself walking into my room to retrieve her, like I did now. It was a little disconcerting sometimes to think that I couldn't be that close to her anymore. I missed the bonding, mostly, since she'd been gone. And at first it was a little difficult to think about my baby growing up. Gosh, now I sounded like one of those old mothers who suffered from empty-nest syndrome. Chuckling at the thought, I turned the *other way* and opened the door to Jasmine's new room. Well, it wasn't all that new, but it still seemed fresh to me.

I found her awake, surprisingly, and playing with the toys in her crib. When she saw me, she began to squeal in delight, and reach out for me. Compared to me, she was so tanned given the fact she just returned from North Carolina with her Father, Juan. I laughed good-naturedly and picked her up. She was so exuberant; she started wriggling around in my arms while she tugged at my now four inch longer hair. It was now straight, and stopped at the center of my back. Looking down, I noticed that my nails had gotten longer, too. It was probably because I actually allowed them to grow lately. I was usually always gnawing them down from stress or boredom or both that I thought they'd be stunned for life. Huh. Apparently I was wrong.

The image of me growing large talons from my nails had me laughing as I handed Jasmine over to my Mother. She took her and watched me with teasing suspicion. "My, my Reina. I haven't seen you this happy in months!"

I rolled my eyes and asked. "Should I check on the pies? They smell like they're ready?"

She smiled thoughtfully and giggled. "Oh, I must have forgotten. Could you please?" I nodded, cheesing, and started toward the oven. Enrique never liked cake, so instead every year my mother baked about a dozen apple cinnamon pies and stuck a candle in each of them. I smiled to myself; my big brother was turning twenty-five and he had grown up so much since then. It wasn't like he had ever jumped out of the LC's yet, but I knew he had a handle on it. After all, he made his territory known to the rival gang last month and ever since no one else has messed with him. His gang members actually respect that he got a job and was doing something with his life—at least that's what he told me. Sighing, I thought of the last time I saw him, and it made me miss him all the more. Shaking away the thought, I quietly turned the oven off and took the two pies out and placed them on the counter to cool. Oh, they looked delicious enough to eat right now! Looking around slyly, I took a spoon and started for the apple-y goodness when my Mother called excitedly from the living room for me. Dropping the spoon, I dashed inside the room and saw something that lifted my heart in joy and pride.

Jasmine wore the pink, Christening-looking dress with a huge smile on her face and sitting complacently in my Mother's arms.

I nearly sobbed when I said, "She's breathtaking..."

"She's a princess." My Mom said smugly.

When I approached them, she held Jasmine out to me; I took her and held her tight to my chest. How could such a tiny girl bring me to tears so easily? Jasmine stopped smiling and wiped a tear from my face.

"No, baby." I giggled reassuringly, "I'm crying because you're so beautiful in that dress."

As if she understood, she smiled and started making contented baby noises. She laid her head against my shoulder, and I cradled her all the way towards the ringing door everyone ignored until I composed myself. When I opened the door, the waterworks came out harder: standing before me was my big brother, tall, full, and healthy. I hugged him for a long moment and whispered, "You're really here!" I'm excited.

"Yeah, I'm here." He chuckled deeply; his voice had gotten so deep, and said, "And you're glowing!"

I giggled from the compliment. Suddenly, there was this short, black, chubby girl with her long hair in a ponytail, and a beautiful smile. I looked at Enrique in confusion.

He drew a deep breath and said to me, "Angela, this is my sister Reina and her daughter Jasmine."

"Hello!" Angela sang, smiling brightly at me.

"Ray, this is Angela Pierce." Ricky paused to share an adoring look with her and whispered, "My fiancée."

Catching a wobbly vain

SUDDENLY, I HEARD MY Mother yelp with joy, and I knew she overheard. Even my stern Father joined her in her gleeful tirade. "Come on inside so I can see my future daughter-in-law! Aren't you guys freezing?" Mom asked. They walked inside, hand in hand, and I shut the door behind them with a smile. My big brother was finally a man now. That thought alone made me want to do a little happy dance.

Jasmine was up now and giggling at the sight of her Uncle whom she hadn't seen in a while. Enrique had his arms outstretched and cooed, "Do you 'member your Uncle Ricky, Yaz?"

Jasmine screamed joyfully and nearly jumped into his arms.

He kissed her on the forehead and looked down at me. I was still crying—yikes—when he walked over to me. He was beaming so brightly it felt as if I needed shades to look at him. "How're things little sister?" He asked me. I shook my head and cleared my face, feeling as young as Jasmine all over again. "Things are good." I replied. After a second I held my hand up and corrected, "Great actually. And you?"

He chuckled and turned to gaze at Angela, who was being harassed with hugs and questions and baby pictures on the sofa with our parents. Ricky sighed, "Better than great. Lovely." *Lovely?* Whoever that girl was was having an awesome affect on my big brother. Sooner or later I would have to thank her. "I know we've only known each other for a little over a month now, but I feel that...that it's right. I don't know Ray; I just know that she's the only one for me." He was smiling fondly at his dream girl, totally making me want to sob with pride for my brother. He playfully punched me on the arm and said, "So what's gotten into you lately? Last time I saw you, you looked like crap, now you look like a model." He beamed at me. "I'm so proud of you, girl. I heard you won that national poetry competition last week. How much did you win?" It wasn't as if he were prying, he was just curious. I cheesed from the pride

I felt from winning that trophy and check. "A thousand."

Ricky released a low whistle and hugged me hard. "I'm so *proud* of you, my girl!" He exclaimed to me in Spanish. I hugged him back and then we parted all too soon. He handed me back my daughter, and glanced at our parents and Angela. He chortled and teased, "I better go save Angela from witnessing a picture of my ugly ass as a baby!" Of course it was only a joke—he was probably the best looking guy in the family. I ran my hand through the head full of hazel curls in Jasmine's hair before I walked up to the four of them and offered gently, "You guys want to go slice the pies now and sing Happy Birthday before Ricky gets any older?" Everyone laughed as we all entered the dining room to see the large display of about two dozen pies neatly laid out on the large table. Each had one candle inside them. My Mom turned to face Angela and explained, "I made one for every wonderful year he has made me proud. Twenty-five pies for my baby boy!"

"Wow." Angela said in her thick Yankee accent, amazed.

My Father patted my brother proudly on the back and said, "That's my boy!" Ricky hugged him, and after that he leaned down low to kiss Angela on the top of her head. I smiled.

"All right, now it's time to sing to the Birthday Boy!" My Mom sang. "Reina, why don't you start us off?" She asked.

I agreed and stopped dead in my tracks at an occurring thought. Oh no! We normally sang the Happy Birthday Song in Spanish, but how would Angela follow along if she didn't know it? The last thing I wanted to do was embarrass her! Panicked I looked down, and said lowly, "How about we sing it in English this year, guys?"

To my utter shock, everyone in the room laughed. Even Jasmine. Angela recovered first, clung to Enrique, and said, "It's all right Reina! I'm a Spanish teacher, go ahead, I can follow along." I was washed with relief when a thought occurred to me. I narrowed my eyes suspiciously and turned to my parents. "How did you guys know before me?" My Mother spoke first, "Why, she just told us in the living room."

Well, damn.

"So where did the two of you meet?" I asked after I polished off the last of my clam chowder. It was later in the morning and my Mom decided to make everyone breakfast. So there we all were, in the living room with our plates/bowls in our laps because the dining room was being occupied.

Enrique and Angela had been sitting close on the love seat, grinning occasionally at each other with so much love in their eyes. Enrique cleared his throat and began, "Well, I was out on the job, when my boss walks up to me and asks if I would like to work on this huge project for one of the nearby schools. He said it was good pay, and heck yeah I agreed to it." He turned and winked at his fiancée before continuing, "The school was being closed off for a month, because it was under construction, so my first day on the job I went busy away with work until something very yellow caught my eye."

Angela slapped him playfully on the arm and she finished, "It was the first day the school closed down, and I was headed toward my classroom to get some files I wanted to go over. I couldn't help but noticed this handsome guy ogling me through the main window instead of the huge rosebush he was supposed to have been working on." She narrowed her eyes suspiciously at him, smiling. "And F.Y.I, I was wearing a yellow *cardigan!*"

"I'd love you even if that thing was turd green. You'll always be beautiful to me." He smiled and finally gave her a quick kiss on the lips. She giggled when they parted. Jasmine laughed out loud in her high chair and started dancing around. We all laughed then, until my Mother called from the kitchen, "Ray! Could you come here, please?"

I excused myself and wandered inside the kitchen where she'd beckoned me. "Yes?"

She had been working on dinner, which was a huge roasted chicken, stuffing, corn, mashed potatoes, mac and cheese, collard greens, fried beans, brownies, and four large pitures of grape Kool-Aid. She was sweating when she said, "Could you go to the store for me and pick up some more eggs? Oh, and bread, too." She pointed to counter. "My purse is on the counter; there's a ten in my wallet. And you can take the car if you'd like."

I grabbed the ten, and started for the door. "Nah, I'll walk. It's a fresh morning." I was wearing pajama pants and my pink night shirt. Looking down, I decided it wasn't working and went upstairs to change. I decided to wear my favorite black leggings and cut off mini skirt. I exchanged my pink shirt for a long sleeved gray one, as I always did, and made my way into the living room.

"Where you going, Ray?" My brother's voice was worried.

I waved my hand, and then went for the coat rack. "The store, Mommy wants some stuff for dinner." When my flight coat was on, I walked up to Jasmine, kissed her on the forehead, and whispered, "I'll be right back, baby." She giggled.

On my way to the store, I stopped and stared down the street I hadn't traveled down in a month:

West Avenue.

Before I could stop myself, I began down the street that led to the one place where I ever *truly* felt comfortable. I had to turn a corner to later find the homey café which I had grown to really like and remembered. The Stream was just on the corner and had this huge window where you could see the customers laughing, eating and having a good time. I hadn't even noticed I was just standing there looking creepily inside the café at the many people who ignored me. I watched longingly as a tall waiter with dreads pulled back into a ponytail handed a giant cup of coffee to a big man with a funny shaped head. The man thanked him, and the waiter smiled, wiped his hands on his pants and finally locked gazes with me. As our eyes held each other, we both froze. My heart was beating so fast; I reacted way too late to the muffled sounding, "Reina!" coming from him inside the building. He maneuvered past the crowds of people inside, trying to make it to the door.

But he was too late.

I turned and ran like hell to my father's store, losing Ross by a few blocks.

Fireworks in the hallway

WHEN I RETURNED HOME, I entered a complete territory of delight. Everyone was laughing and sharing stories of the past; having a good-old time.

Until they saw me...

My brother stood up instantly, "Are you okay, Reina?" I nodded and rushed inside the kitchen. I sat the groceries on the kitchen counter and clutched my hands tightly on the edge of it. I could feel my knuckles turning white from the strain, but it was all I could do to stop shaking and to slow my heart rate.

"Was it Juan?" My Mother's voice came from behind me all of a sudden. When I opened my mouth to speak, I exhaled deeply. I was holding my breath.

I gulped, "No, he's still in school." I felt her hand on my shoulder then.

"Then who?"

"Nobody!" I snapped. I composed myself and stood straighter. "I'm sorry." I was shaking my head in order to clear it. Ever since that time between Ross and me, I've tried my best avoiding him. Even in French class, I moved my seat far away from him. Well, it wasn't as if I didn't notice the looks he's been giving me, always so full of sadness. Never once had I met those gazes. Never.

Not until today.

I didn't have anything against him, I mean; he was still the same goofy guy I'd met last month. But I wasn't avoiding him for him—I did it for me. After that afternoon with Ross, he kissed me on the lips, and left. And after he left I still had that cheap, shameful, empty feeling. Apparently, neither the booze nor sex could numb that pain I was still feeling. So, that day, I closed my eyes and sworn off all guys forever. It was just too much heartache juggling all those problems. Yes, I admitted it, all they brought were problems. Ross— physical, Juan—parental, and Emilio—emotional/mental...

Emilio. I smiled at the thought of him. We weren't back together, but ever since the gang fight, he had become one of my best friends. I guess we both realized it was for the best that we kept our relationship completely platonic. With Juan, I only dealt with him where Jasmine was concerned. With Ross, I decided to totally cast him away from my life. With Emilio, however, he was the only exception. I mean, the guy was my first love and boyfriend. No matter how upset I got with him, there was no way I wanted him completely out of my life. *"I must stick with you..."*

My Mother nodded, kissed me on the cheek, and reached for the groceries. As she un-bagged them, she glanced up at me and smiled. "Want some clam chowder?" Her smile was actually hopeful.

Her kindness nearly brought tears to my eyes.

Blinking them away, I shook my head. "No, Ma. I just had breakfast—thanks though."

She reached her hand out to cup my cheek. "I love you, Reina."

I gave her a weak smile, "I love you, too, Mom." It was such an emotional moment. Before I could stop myself, I hugged the hell out of her. She patted my back and said lowly, "I just wanted you to know that. We all love you, baby."

I pulled back to look her in the eyes. "I know, Ma."

She shook her head, and continued in Spanish, "I know your Father and I haven't been around a lot. You know, him dealing with so much business and me with my speech classes and all. I just want you to know that we're not being away from you on purpose. We're doing this to help your future." She gave my cheek one last pat and scooted me from the kitchen. She didn't want anyone peeking on her, "special dinner". I was grinning when I finally went into the living room to join Enrique, Angela, and my Father who was holding Jasmine, they were totally LOL-ing as I walked in.

"So, when I turned the eye on, this really big flame shoots out, and that's how I got this scar!" Enrique said goofily as he rolled his sleeve up to reveal a dark brown patch. It was about the size of a dollar bill. It was an old scar, but it still shocked me. "Yikes!" I gasped. Angela ducked down and placed a kiss on it. Ricky was cheesing so hard. He looked up at me then, and said simply. "It was no big deal." He leaned back and draped a protective arm around Angela.

"So, are you okay, Ray?" My Father asked. He looked truly concerned, even though he bounced an infant on his knee. I nodded and extended my arms out to Jasmine. She looked worried too as my Dad handed her over to me. I stood up, and started up the stairs. "Where you goin, Ray?" Ricky asked me worriedly.

"I need to make a call. I'll come right back, I swear." I promised. He looked doubtful and nodded. I hope I didn't upset him. With a silent Jasmine, I entered my room. With her in my lap, I grabbed my Blackberry and speed-dialed Luz Lopez's number.

It rang twice before a zealous voice answered, "Hey, Ray!" Her tone made me chuckle. "Why," I began, "You're awful chipper!"

She laughed. What got into her? Before I could ask her, she exclaimed. "Oh! Tell Ricky I said Happy Birthday." I nodded, feeling stupid because I knew she couldn't see it.

Laughing at myself, I added, "Oh, guess what?"

"Juan, fell off the planet?" She asked me, aware that Juan was never my favorite person in the world. Smiling I corrected her, "No. I'm afraid if that does happen, Yaz would be quite upset." I could practically hear her pouting through the phone. "But what I *do* have to tell you, is that Ricky is engaged! Can you believe that?"

She was silent for a moment before realization struck her. "Oh! Ricky as in *Enrique?* Your brother? Tell him I said congrats!"

Grinning with pride for my brother I agreed. "Sure."

There was a pause before Luz said. "Is Yazzy there now? Tell her auntie Luz said hey!"

I looked down at the silent child in my arms and placed the phone to her ear. She smiled at the gesture and started babbling. "Tell Luz you said hello, baby." She grabbed the phone from me and shoved it in her mouth. "Ah! No, don't do that. It's gross." I took the phone from her, wiped away the slob, and spoke into it. "Sorry, she just tried to eat my phone."

Luz laughed. "So, did you hear about the Halloween dance next Friday?"

How could I not? It was only advertised all over the school. "Yeah, I heard about it. What are you going as?"

Her answer was instant. "A French maid." My eyes bugged at the image of my friend in a skimpy mini skirt and push up bra.

"Uh, ew!" I shuddered from the sight.

"What?" She asked innocently. "The skirt's gonna stop a little ways above my knees."

I smirked. "Mm-hm. And what about cleavage?"

She was totally laughing out loud then. "That's a given! But back to important matters, are you going?" I decided to say no when an image of her face came to mind the last time I was at the café. The disappointment in her face was so raw it was tangible. So, choosing not to go down that road again I concurred. "Yes! Will you have a date?" Now *that* I truly didn't know of.

I shrugged and answered, "Maybe, I don't know. I guess not."

"Well, I think Emilio's going. Try and persuade him to ask you out."

"Okay, sure, I'll try. Anything else?" I said quickly. I didn't want to talk about guys right now. Jasmine wriggled in my arms and began to fuss. "Ah, I'll have to talk to you later, Luz. All right?"

"Okay. See you later." And then there was the dial tone.

My face contorted at the smell of poop. I looked down into her crying eyes and said, "Did someone just go to the bathroom?"

She wriggled again. "Okay, okay. I'm getting the diapers now." I picked her up and started for her room. I laid her carefully down on the changing bed and pulled her dress up. When she was cleaned, I latched a diaper on her and she started giggling. "Yes, I know! You're all clean now." I laid her down in her crib, and turned to throw away the smelly diaper when the smell finally registered with me. I dropped it and ran for the bathroom toilet. For a long time I just sat there on the bathroom floor thinking and puking my brains out.

High tide and low riders

I BRUSHED MY TEETH. It was the most necessary thing to do since there were tidbits of puke between them. When I dried my hands on my skirt, I opened the door to a frowning Angela Pierce. I shifted my eyes from her gaze intentionally and started to walk back down the hall.

When I reached Jasmine's door, I heard her call, "Hey, Reina!"

Damn. I thought I was free, but I guess not. I cleared my throat and responded weakly. "Um, yeah?"

She glanced around as if she were being watched and came closer to me. "Are you okay, sweetie? You sounded sick from inside there."

I looked around, too. "Y-Yes." This was so uncomfortable. I had nothing against her, but there was no way I was in the mood for talking. I was afraid I'd puke again. "Um, I have to change Jasmine." She nodded and I rushed inside the room and shut the door. My heart was beating really fast. Where the hell did that come from? I changed my daughter's poop all time, and never did I actually get physically sick. Maybe it was a bug? I don't know, maybe it was just because I'd been thinking of last month—which pretty much was the worst month of my life so far. Yeah, that was it. Overwhelmed, the tears started falling out of nowhere; Jasmine whined and reached out to me. Fully crying now; I approached my daughter, picked her up, and held her tight. We both cried in each other's arms until I heard my mother call, "Dinner!" from downstairs. I cleared my eyes and carried a subdued Jasmine downstairs with me. The laughter automatically died down at the sight of me. Their gazes were flickering back and forth between me and Jasmine.

Both of our eyes were tearstained.

My Mother came up to me and said worriedly, "Are you guys...is there something I should know?"

I shook my head diligently. How and why would I tell them I had a nervous breakdown? Just minutes ago I appeared perfectly fine...*glowing* to my brother. Now how would I explain that I was going crazy?

I cleared my throat. "You said dinner was ready?"

"Reina, are you okay?" I didn't know who asked me that, but suddenly I felt sick again. This time I forced it down, handed Jasmine to my Mother, and started for the kitchen. The smell of the delicious food was tantalizing, but it made me sick at the same time. Unable to handle myself, I grabbed a spoon and rushed the baked macaroni and cheese. The cheese hit the bottom of my stomach, and it screamed out that it didn't want it, but I continued anyway. I was starving but I wanted to puke at the same time. It was a horrible feeling, but I thought if I just kept eating then the pain would go away.

"Reina!" Cried a voice from behind me. When I turned around, my mouth was full of cheesy noodles. Everyone was staring at me, gaping. My Father just looked crazy mad, and my Mother was sobbing. No doubt over spoiling Enrique's surprise dinner. "I'm so sorry..." I blubbered over the food in my mouth and the tears in my eyes. A wave of nausea hit me like a sack of bricks and I rushed to the kitchen sink to begin throwing my guts up. When I finished, there was puke all over the dishes that lay in the sink. Crying, I dashed from the kitchen. Grabbing my jacket, I threw my Mom's slippers on from the living room and was out the door. I never changed my clothes earlier, so it was no problem to throw my shoes on and get away. When I was finally outside I started to run. I had no idea where I was going, or how I ended up near this abandoned warehouse. There was a streetlight on near the cold stone-like wall; feeling hopeless and totally depleted I leaned against it, and made no move to go even when it started to rain.

The bliss of gray

TWO DAYS PASSED AND I found myself...emotionless? Yeah, that's it. I was just drained that I had no idea how I'd managed to make it to school. Enrique and Angela left with most of the left over pies, and unease toward me. Ever since my "episode" I found that my family had shunned me. Well, that's what it felt like. My Mother joined a book club and was balancing that and her speech classes. My Father was still always away every day at either the store or the Laundromat, and the times he was here he barely spoke to me. Yep, so it was safe to say that I was back where I'd started.

Alone, numb, and confused.

On the other hand though, Ross was making an über effort to ignore me. Even though this was a time where I *really* needed a friend. Luz was gone to only God knows where for the past two days but she left me a butt load of messages I didn't feel like answering to. And I felt extremely alone. No, abandoned.

On the upside though, Emilio was back in school walking upright and looking better than ever. We never got a chance to speak to each other though, mostly because all his classes were on an entirely other floor than mine. His was north, and mines were south. And that was just the way things were.

Now, I was at my locker looking in there for whoever knows what. Really, I was just staring at it, unmoving. I could feel the tears coming on when someone finally nudged my arm.

"You okay, babe?" It was Emilio. It had to be, because I knew that Italian accent anywhere. He closed my locker and took my backpack from me.

I sniffled and met his gaze. "I'm fine." I said and thought for a bit. "You should go though. If you don't you'll be late for your class." I started to take my bag from him when moved my hand away.

"Nah, I got it. Plus, you look like you've just been through the wire. What happened?" Again, another *loaded* question.

"Don't ask questions you don't want answers to, Milio."

He shrugged, seemingly unaffected by my callousness. "I know you're in a bad mood, but I was wondering if you wanted to go to the Halloween dance with me on Friday?" Shit, I'd forgotten about that. Again, I reminded myself that I was going for Luz. Speaking of which... "Milio, where is Luz? Do you know?"

He fidgeted. "She had to go to Georgia, because her brother who lived there...his girlfriend was killed in a driveby."

I flinched. So that's what all those messages were for? I felt so much like a bad person, maybe it wasn't meant to be for me to have friends? Or even associates for that matter, because in the end I'd probably end up doing what I always do. Screw them over.

We reached my fourth period, which was French class (bummer), and that's when he handed my backpack to me, kissed me on my forehead, whispered, "I'll swing by around eight," and left.

My cheeks heated the instant I realized the entire class saw it—including a sullen-looking Ross Nolan...

School was over in a flash and I was out of there just as quick. Again, French class had been killing me, and I was dying for some clam chowder. Even though, every time I thought of food I'd gain ten pounds, and puke it back up. Ugh, it wasn't fair. Gosh, I hadn't felt this hopeless since—

Shit! No. No. No. No! I couldn't be...it didn't make sense...how...why...when? The signs were all coming together. Right then, I wasn't certain, but it was closest thing to a diagnosis: I was—

The sound of a car horn interrupted my thinking and pissed me off. Exasperated, I turned to see a smooth looking Navigator pulling up by me. I looked up and down the street I was walking to make sure there were no witnesses.

Ross exited the car and walked over to where I stopped. As always, he was looking as luscious as ever. He was wearing a black sweater over some black Sean Jean Jeans. His hair had gotten longer and he kept it in a loose ponytail to the back of his head. Damn me, my body was already reacting to him! He stood before me now and spoke over the loud, biting, winds. "You should get in the car—it's freezing, Reina." Narrowing my eyes, I did the unthinkable.

I slapped him as hard as I could. "I don't want your ride! Your *ride* was what got me in so much trouble in the first place!" I screamed.

Ross recovered from the blow as if I hadn't delivered one at all and said lowly. Dangerously. "Get in the car, right now!" I widened my eyes. *Oh, no he didn't!* I pushed him, which of course he didn't budge. He just looked angrier. Taking my shoulders in his hands, he shook me and said, "Why won't you just talk to me?"

"You just shook m—" Before I could get the words out, puke came spewing out of my mouth. Ross jumped back before it could hit him, which I wanted it to, but thought it immature. So I turned and threw up on the brick wall that was behind me. Ross came up behind me then and started rubbing my back. "It's okay. Just breathe in and out." I did, and it helped, so I stood straighter and leaned against the wall for support. I wiped my mouth and said raggedly, "I just want a little peace, Ross. Is that too much to ask?" He didn't answer, just led me to his car. All the fight left me, so I could no longer move or run—just follow. When he buckled me up, he got in and started the engine. On the drive he asked me in a thick tone, "What was that, Reina?" I was so weak I could barely hear my phone screaming at me. Sighing, I answered it and greeted, "Huh?" It was more of a groan, but the panicked voice took it anyway. "Ray?" My Mother's voice was thick with tears. I frowned, "What is it?"

"It's Jasmine!" She cried. And her next words made me want to die. "She's in the hospital!"

I dropped the phone and screamed, "Take me to the hospital!" At Ross who was just nearing my house. Without hesitation, he gunned it all the way to Pegrams Hospital for Youth. On the drive however, I was crying and wailing and blubbering prayers for my baby. Oh shit! How could I let this happen?

"Tell me what happened?" Ross asked frantically. After I hesitated he demanded, "Reina!"

"My daughter's in the hospital!" I cried.

"Oh, shit!" He shouted and gunned it even faster. Before I knew it, we were in the hospital's parking lot when he parked, helped me out, and we both started running toward the door. If a truck ran me over right then and there, I wouldn't have even bothered being scared. I'd have welcomed it.

Soul searching in a brothel

"REINA!" MY MOTHER CALLED me from the waiting room. I was panting so hard when I stopped beside her. Ross was beside me in an instant, and my Mother didn't pay him any mind. She had a Kleenex in her hand and she was praying in rapid Spanish.

"Where is she?" I asked, trying but failing to keep my voice level. I was shouting.

"Ma'am?" A feminine voice came from behind me. I believed it to be one of the nurses available to tell me to calm down. How could she dare do that? My daughter wasn't even a year old yet, and she was in the damn hospital!

"You bitch!" I turned around and screeched. I started to pounce on her, until a set of strong arms wound around my waist to hold me back.

"Let the doctor explain, Queen." Ross soothed. The woman's eyes were rounded in astonishment. She was a short Latina woman, with a chart in her hands that she was studying now.

"So you're the mother?" She pointed to me with her pen. What the hell was she so nonchalant about? Did she care that my daughter was in here?

Scoffing, I started for her again.

Ross still held me though. I shrugged out of his hold and said curtly, "Where the hell is my daughter?"

Apparently, the doctor hadn't noticed—or just ignored—my coldness and extended her hand out to me. "Dr. Baxter." She greeted. I just glared at it until she placed it back at her side. Sighing, she continued. "Jasmine Reyes..." She was focusing on her charts, reciting, "Female, Hispanic, and hazel eyes."

"I already fucking know that!" I exploded. It was pissing me off that she was spouting nonsense and not leading me towards Jasmine's room. Dr. Baxter just looked at me sympathetically. "It's pneumonia. Apparently, we ran some tests and found that she retained all the necessary symptoms."

"Pneumonia? What?" I inquired, saddened now. How could that be? My parents' house was always warm—hot even. I mean, there was central heating there. Which brought me back to that question: how could that be?

"How could that be?" My Mother repeated from my internal debating.

The doctor just shook her head, frowning. "From what you told me of Jasmine's current environment, there's no way to really tell for sure. Are you certain that she hasn't been outside too long or anything? Left a door open? A window cracked?"

"NO!" I roared. No, sobbed. Well, it was a mixture of both really. I was now sitting in one of the chairs available in the waiting room, my head in my hands.

"Reina! *Miel?*" Juan's voice reverberated easily through the busy hall. I looked up at him; when our eyes met he ran over to me and got on his knees. So now, he was kneeling in front of me as I sat— my gaze low and crying. "Oh, baby! I'm so sorry. I was in class when your Mom called me and told me what happened." There was a heart wrenching bleakness to his voice. His arms were around me then, and I found myself hugging him tight against me. He wasn't crying, but his hands were rubbing my back. It wasn't a sexual gesture, but a friendly one that I needed more than anything. When I pulled back from him, I blubbered, "Our daughter has *pneumonia,* Juan!" Suddenly, Juan was hovering over Dr.

Baxter, who was watching and waiting patiently in the background. "Take me to her. Now!"

"Are you the Father?" She asked. Her eyes were alternating between Ross and him.

"Yes." He ignored Ross and continued, "I want to see my daughter."

"Well," She began. "The ICU is limited to only two people a time—"

"What?" Juan, My Mom, even Ross, and I shrieked. Dr. Baxter held her hands up in surrender.

"Yes. We're only keeping her there until the infection clears out of her lungs. Now, we'll allow the parents entrance first." We started walking down the narrow hall, until we reached a purely white door that read, INTENSIVE CARE UNIT on it. Juan and I shared worried gazes. When Dr. Baxter opened the door what I saw made my knees give out.

Jasmine was lying in this big, clear tube like thing. There were two openings that molded into gloves so that we could touch her without spreading any germs. She was so still it scared the hell out of me. Even when she was sleeping, she was never *that* motionless. Juan caught me before I could fall, and helped me over to stand by Jasmine. The doctor decided to leave us alone and left. She told us to inform her when we were finished. But that was the problem; I didn't want to go anywhere. I wanted...I wanted...hell, with all this heartache, death. I couldn't bear to live if my baby ever passed away before me. Guy problems I could deal with, but my daughter dying? No way could I live through that pain.

No way would I want to.

Juan helped me erect myself, and reached his hand through one of the gloves to stroke her cheek. "Don't worry, baby. You're gonna be all right, I promise. Daddy's not gonna' leave you, I'll—" His words broke into pained sobs. Placing his other hand to his eyes, he started to wipe away the tears. That sight alone made me want to bang my head against the solid walls. I was sitting in a chair now, just gawking at nothing in particular. I was all cried out.

When Juan and I exited the ICU the entire gang was waiting for us in the waiting room: My Mother and Father, Enrique and Angela, Ross and Emilio. They all were weeping hard. Hell, they were probably the loudest things in the entire pediatrics center. I was so glad that they were all here supporting Jasmine in her time of need. I smiled weakly at all of them, looking, but not really seeing them. Everything was just so numb. I zombied over to a chair and sat down. "Oh, that poor baby!" Angela sobbed lowly to Enrique. He just nodded, silent tears coursing down his face, and embraced her as tightly as he could, so it looked. My parents were up next to see Jasmine. Throughout the rest of the day that's how things were rotating. My family was visiting my sick daughter in couples in her room.

It was around midnight when Dr. Baxter advised us to go home and come back the following morning. I pleaded with her so I could stay. I didn't want to leave her side at all. "Please!" I entreated her. I was on my knees then, hugging her legs like a petulant child. Someone helped me up and held me against their chest to right me. "Shh, just breathe." Emilio said in my ear. I relaxed a degree and decided not to fight anymore. Dr. Baxter took hesitant steps back, until she finally turned and paced away. Emilio helped me back in my chair, and I began to slump. I wanted to bawl my eyes out, but again, I was too hollow for that. For the past few minutes, Emilio just held me close to his chest and quietly rocked me. "I don't want to live without Jasmine, Emilio. That's torture." I whispered, barely hearing myself. He leaned back and wiped his face of the tears he'd been shedding. "Now, Reina—"

"No." I said distantly. "I. Don't. Want. To. Live."

Emilio grabbed my cheeks and peered into my eyes. "I won't let that happen." He said surly, and pulled me in for a smoldering kiss. The rest of the family was busy with consoling each other or down the hall standing outside Jasmine's door. The kiss was fierce and consoling all at the same time. I could taste his tears.

The kiss was salty, sweet and ended all too abruptly at the grim sounding voice. "Reina, I need to talk to you." Ross's voice came to me like a whip. I pulled away suddenly from Emilio. His eyes were still closed, as if he were savoring that kiss, and when his eyes opened they flashed cold hate.

Standing up, he shoved Ross in the chest and said dangerously, "Get the *fuck* out of my face before you get yourself in trouble." My eyes widened at what was about to happen:

Emilio was about to fight Ross in the pediatrics center.

Belly dancing on cloud five

ROSS DIDN'T SPEAK—HE ACTED. With a strength I had no idea he had, Ross shoved Emilio so hard he practically flew across the room, crashing into the wall. "Ay, yo, don't you *fucking* touch me unless you gotta fuckin death wish homie!" He bellowed and stalked after Emilio. Suddenly, guards were there, and were hauling the two of them outside. After they had been thrown out, I ran after them. Ross and Emilio were circling each other like animals in the wild.

I reached the center of them quickly and screamed. "Stop it now!"

Ross obeyed and put his hands over his face. "You're right. I didn't move here to do this shit." He breathed. Emilio was just standing there, glaring daggers at Ross as he approached me. Miraculously, Ross was placated when he asked, "Please, Queen? I really need to talk to you."

I opened my mouth to answer when I heard Emilio say, "Tell that *Rasta bitch* to get the hell out of here, Ray!"

Then Ross lost it again. "Yo, shut the hell up before I go over there and wipe that smirk off your face, boy."

"Oh yeah? Come over and try it— pussy!"

Ross advanced toward Emilio, both yelling and going for each other's throats. I felt queasy again, and inhaled the sharp winds. What I said next would end any friendship I had with Emilio and Ross too. I laid a hand over my stomach and prayed to God for strength before I yelled. "I'm pregnant, Ross!"

Both guys stopped and turned to gape at me.

"What?" Enrique's angry voice came from behind me. Turning around, I noticed my entire family standing there, gaping as the two guys fighting had been.

Emilio looked disgusted before he turned on his heel and walked away.

Clawing to the top

EVERYTHING WENT, SUDDENLY, VERY still. Everyone froze, and it wasn't because of the harsh winds. I stood in the center of the parking lot—a direct split between Ross and my family. The nausea came back, almost the most intense ever, but I choked it down while I debated what to do. Go after Emilio, and tell him how sorry I was? That any of this happened? Just when he was starting to love me again, I just had to go and ruin it by getting knocked up. Again. Ironically, it was like I was reliving everything from ten months ago, only that I was suffering alongside Ross Nolan instead of Juan Cruz. I could feel the tears prick my eyes; I had to do this…to face the music. Besides, I was so tired of running, and holding the pain inside—of feeling so got-damn numb. No matter how much effort it took, I stood there, calmly, and forced myself not to run after Emilio. I held my chin high and stared firmly at my family. I took a deep breath. "Yes. I-I think I'm pregnant." I blinked back tears and turned to Ross. "And it's yours. I'm sure of that." Ross was just standing there, not looking at me, but off into the distance somewhere. His expression was a mixture of confusion, pain, and sadness. It hurt my heart to think I was causing him so much of that anguish—causing my family so much of it, too. "I'm so sorry, Ross, I—"

He held his hand up to silence me and started for his car.

I would have moved to stop him, but found myself frozen. I closed my eyes, unable to bear the sight of anybody else walking out of my life. When Ross was long gone, I turned to my family and yelled over the winds, "I'm so sorry guys..."

"Why do you always have to *do* shit like this?" Enrique asked angrily, clenching and unclenching his fists. Angela was just looking deeply sad as she stood silently at his side. Enrique looked up to me, and it was there where I saw the pain in his eyes. "I try so hard to protect you Reina." He shook his head and took Angela's hand. "I-I just can't take this anymore." He pulled his fiancée with him towards a blue Chevrolet—hers, I guessed. When I heard my brother speedily drive off, a loud sob racked me.

It was Juan's turn to chew me out. "Really, Reina? At a time like this?" He gestured toward the hospital doors next to him. His face was blotchy and pale from the tears he'd been shedding for Jasmine. He reminding me of that nearly sent me on my knees in agony. Each word someone spoke to me was like a dagger stabbing me in the heart. Juan shook his head, sniffed, then said in a deadly tone that had me crying out, "If it wasn't for that little girl in there, I'd want *nothing* to do with you." Juan stalked to his blue-flamed Lamborghini and sped off—leaving behind only my parents now. My Mother slowly approached me and began to rub my back in a soothing gesture. "Come on, baby. It's time to go home now." And the weirdest thing of all was when my always-so-stern Father walked up to my side and hugged me. I hugged him fiercely back and my Mother encircled her arms around the both of us.

For a while we stood there, weeping over so many things.

Prayers for sanity

"YOU FUCKED UP, REINA. No doubt." A deep voice resonated from...somewhere around me. I couldn't see; there was so much darkness. I could feel something pricking my skin, like feline whiskers or something. The strange sensation was irritating my skin all over, and whatever the heck it was—I knew I had to get away from it. "Get off of me!" I screamed out in the darkness. I was scared, and I knew I was not alone. Looking around frantically, I searched the dark place. There was nothing to see, only voices. Ugh, the prickling was growing more intense and I was certain that there was something on me. *Scratching* me. I flung my hand out in the abyss and felt nothing but a slight air pressure. Wherever I was—was some sort of confinement. "You shouldn't have ever done it, Reina! You should be ashamed." There was another voice I knew. For some reason, I just couldn't place it. It was as if I had wandered into a land of the unknown, yet everyone was acquainted with you instead of vice versa. Like amnesia. "I'm sorry!" I answered. Wherever these voices were coming from, I wanted them to go back. I didn't need this right now. Not with so much going on like...what the hell was going on, anyway?

And out of the darkness came a shrill scream that made me remember. The deafening wails were coming from Jasmine—I recognized her voice anywhere. She just kept screaming, and screaming, and screaming...

"Stop!" I said weakly.

"You whore!"

"You should be sent away!"

"No one wants a nobody like you!"

And then there were just more screams. I recognized the voices as a mixture of people: Emilio, Ross, Juan, Enrique...

Then I realized what was happening. I wiped the tears that were falling freely down my face and shouted over the screams and insults. "Shut up! I'm not a bad person and it's time you've seen that!" I had no idea where the strength or words were coming from, but I went with it. "It's time you've *seen* that!" I screamed. Then everything was silent. Eerily silent until a sarcastic voice cut in. "And how will you do that without light?"

Suddenly, the darkness faltered and I opened my eyes to a bright light.

"Reina? Are you okay?" A gentle, feminine, voice penetrated the haze that I was in to reveal a sad-looking Luz hovering over me. Her eyes were red and I could tell that she had been crying. Suddenly alert, I jolted upright, to find myself in my room, in my bed. "Oh, Ray!"

She hugged me tightly then, I barely returned it as I asked, "What's wrong?" My heart was beating so fast, I had to strain to hear her all the way.

She looked around nervously and replied, "I heard about everything...Mrs. Reyes said that you might have been angry that she told me—and that I should come up here to see how you were doing." She studied my face. "You don't look too good. And hey." She nudged me in the arm. "I'm sorry about Jas—"

"Aren't you supposed to be in school?" I asked quickly. I didn't want to hear any of it, just to relive the pain of yesterday. I couldn't bear it.

Luz smiled faintly and said, "I took the day off to see how you were doing. Besides, there was so much that happened in Georgia these past three days. I needed to see my best friend for a while. My parents said they didn't mind."

I nodded. "Okay."

"Oh, and I know you're hungry!" She said, shooting for joyfulness, but failing. I smiled; it didn't meet my eyes from what I could tell, and gulped. She reached past me, picked up a bowl from my desk, and sat it gently into my lap. Handing me a spoon she said hopefully, "Clam chowder?"

"Thank you." My stomach roared with anticipation for the food. And I started to ravage it, too, when a memory assailed me. Ross walking into my room with a mug in his hands— smiling. He sat down beside me and started to feed me clam chowder. I remembered finding it very sexy and afterward—

Torture. That's what happened afterward. An action that cost me, so very much, yet lasted so little. The shame and guilt came back and—

"Oh, it's okay. Don't cry..." Luz was wiping my tears away. She took the bowl from me and asked, "You're not hungry?"

Hell yes. "No." I blubbered.

She nodded and put the bowl back. We sat there for a few minutes when she finally stood and said, "I guess

I'll just put this back downstairs then." She grabbed the bowl and started for the door. I ground my teeth in fear over what would happen next. I sighed and prepared for the rejection. "Luz!" I called after her at the doorway. The door was open, but at that point I didn't give a damn who heard me anymore. She turned around and asked, "Hmm?"

I gulped and continued. "I'm pregnant...if you wanted to know." I decided to just lay everything out on the table with hope that she wouldn't reject me. I clenched my eyes shut and prayed for more strength to deal with my best friend of three years walking out on me like everyone else had. My heartbeat sped up.

Luz turned around slowly and asked distantly, "What did you just say?"

I was right, she resented me. "You remember Ross, right? The guy—"

"Of course I remember who the hell he is Reina!" She screeched. I flinched from the unexpected noisiness. Well, I deserved it. I got out of bed then and stood in front of her. "Luz?" She was staring at nothing now. Like she was frozen...

When she spoke her words were low...bleak. Shaking her head vigorously she started talking really fast. "Whydidn'tyoutellme...weweresupposedtobe-friends...Ithought..."

"Luz!" I called frantically. She was looking me in my eyes now. Her eyes were glassy and withered looking—like she lived through a thousand truths. Her arms were around me then; I hugged her back this time when she mumbled, "Did you guys...use protection?" And just as I had with my parents, Luz and I stood there and wept quietly for a while before I answered her. When I pulled back to look her in the eyes I said, "The-The...well...it sort of, um, broke." I assumed it was obvious what "it" was when she gave me a knowing look and nodded. Reaching up, she wiped her tears away and said sadly, "I feel like we're not friends anymore. Like you're pushing me away..." She sniffled and her gaze was weary from crying. "We're still friends right?"

I hugged her tightly and said, "Luz, you're actually one of the few people in this world I love." She smiled and I did too when I gave her a playful jab on the shoulder, "Girl, you know I *lurve* you!"

Luz threw her head back and laughed.

Before I knew it, Friday rolled around and school was over. I had been walking around school—no, *zombying* would be a better word for it—not really feeling anything at all. I just felt so traumatized since...I don't even know when the hell it began; I just knew that there was no way I could get out of it. I began to accept the fact that things were like they were and that it was as unchanging as I was. I was walking home thinking of so many things—Emilio, mostly. God, it sucked to face the reality of things—I was still in love with him. And yes it hurt to realize that I was the reason that he dropped out of school. That I was the reason that Ross went back to his normal life—having fun and joking around with friends. It was as if he didn't know about the fact that I was carrying his kid, or just plain ignored it. It hurt to see how things and people were changing and how I was the only one unable to move on. Now I felt like the odd girl out.

When I finally made it across the street near my house, I noticed someone in the shadows. Like a blotchy shadow in the darkness of the corner. I didn't know what made me go over to check it out, but before I knew it I found myself calling out, "Hello? Is someone there?" I slowly approached the blotch and it began to cringe away, as if it were deciding to run or not. "Hello?" I repeated, scared now.

"Go away!" The raspy voice demanded. He sounded old and wizened. Every instinct in my body told me to get the hell out of there, but stupidly, I kept forward. Besides what did I have to lose? It wasn't as if if I died that anyone would grieve. Hell, *I* wouldn't even feel sorry for me. I had caused everyone so much wrong that I doubt anyone would—

"Go away Reina!" At the mention of my name I knew immediately who it was. I put a hand up to my mouth to muffle the gasp that escaped me when he stepped into the light. He was wearing a hoodie that was pulled over his head. I swallowed the lump in my throat and said, "Emilio...?" It was more of a whisper really, but suddenly he pulled on his hoodie to make sure to cover his face completely. I shook my head, "No, let me see your face." He cowered away as if I'd punch him if he did otherwise. Frustrated, I marched up to him and yanked the pull-over down. My eyes bugged at the sight of him. He hadn't shaved since I last saw him at the hospital—which was two days ago. He smelled sort of musty, and his hair was all wet and shaggy looking.

Whoever this man was was not Emilio. Not *my* Emilio.

He took a deep breath and said calmly, "I didn't want you to see me like this." When I wouldn't say anything he threw his hood up quickly and started away. I held him firmly by the arm and said between clenched teeth. "Stop! Let me take care of you." He shook his head vigorously and shrugged out of my grasp. I grabbed him more forcefully and yanked him down to meet my glare. *"Let. Me. Take. Care. Of. You!"* I demanded hopelessly. My voice was strong yet weak at the same time, like me. Looking closer, I saw the tears in his eyes, "You hurt me bad Reina." He angrily wiped at the tears on his face and started down the street. I didn't bother to stop him this time because I knew that he was gone for good now. There was nothing else I could say to keep him by my side.

"Oh shit." I whispered, stunned at what I saw the moment I walked through the door of my parents house. There was, of course, no one home which left me even more surprised as to what I saw. When I approached the bright, white, embroidered gown I actually had to force myself not to swoon at the beauty of it. It was hanging on the coat rack near the front door, and looking closely I noticed the lime green post-it attached to the plastic covering outside the dress. Peeling it off, I frowned at what it said,

"For my baby girl. I picked this up at the mall yesterday while you were sleeping. Go out and have a good time—be a teenager for a while." -Mom.

I chuckled at that. Yeah, right—me, a normal teenager? Shaking my head I took the dress carefully from the rack and rushed upstairs. I sat it on my bed and stared at it. Should I go through with this? I felt so guilty having a good time when Jasmine and Emilio were going through hell. Should I go to this dance? I paced my bedroom floor before I decided. Again, that familiar queasiness—and not from the pregnancy—roiled through me at the thought of hurting Luz. I couldn't do that, but...

Ugh, okay, so I guess I had to go. But still, it didn't assuage the guilt I felt at the thought of partying while everyone around me was so sad. And then I thought of how my parents had been treating me these past few days. My mother was only trying to help cheer me up at every turn, and I rejected her. My ever-so-stern Father often told me of how much he loved me no matter what. Deep inside, it touched my heart to finally hear it after all those years of uncertainty. I swallowed the urge to throw up, and studied the clock that hung on my wall. Five o' clock. The Halloween Dance began at seven-thirty. Great, that gave me just enough time to do what I'd been too weak to do in two days. I fished my Blackberry out of my back pocket and dialed the number. After a thousand rings, I could hear Enrique's deep voice asking to politely leave a message at the tone. I hissed in frustration and obliged. "Ricky." I said, my voice trembling. "I just wanted to call and tell you how sorry I am about Wednesday." Silence answered me. I exhaled sharply at the unfairness of my brother, and decided that I deserved it. "Well, I guess I deserve this, huh?" I hadn't realized I said that out loud until a smooth Yankee accent answered on the other end. "No, you don't deserve this Reina—no one does."

"Angela?" I asked, confounded for only a second. "Is that you?"

She scoffed. "Of course. And by the way, don't feel ashamed to tell me if you hear any other female at this number, okay?" I chuckled at that—knowing she was only being paranoid to cheer me up. "I will."

"Good. Now, back to what I was saying, I spoke to your brother about the other night. He's still upset with you, but I'll just give it a few romantic dinners and a back-rub—and he'll be harmless."

I hesitated, then asked, "I-Is he there now?"

"Nah, he's at work hon. But I'll give him a message if you want, okay?" She asked- her tone friendly.

I smiled weakly and said. "No, it's okay. I-I have to get ready for this thing in a few hours. Thanks, though."

She sounded a little worried. "All right, have a good night then."

There goes my hero

"WHOA! YOU'RE SO BEAUTIFUL—LIKE Cinderella." It was eight o' clock when Luz decided to pick me up for the dance. Luz assured me that Joey was arriving with some of his friends later on, so that she could come with me. I knew it was sympathy, but accepted it because it was all in good will. She meant no harm by it. For the first time in forever, I could feel myself blush at the compliment.

"Thank you so much. You're looking...special in that costume." I said as I climbed inside the black *Range Rover*. She looked down at her outfit, her hands firmly on the steering wheel. As promised, she wore the short skirted French maid suit. Her hair was done in a pile of black curls that sat at the top of her head. Honestly, just looking at her face you'd guess that she was about twelve. Those big eyes just seemed so angelic. We were on the road by the time she glanced at me and said something I didn't expect her to say. "Ross is gonna be there. I just thought you should know." Her eyes went quickly to my stomach then she turned back to the road. I nodded and blurted. "It's not as if he cares about me—us, even." My hand flew protectively to my stomach. Looking down, I wondered what it would look like. Would it have light brown curls like me, or dark ones like Ross? Would "it" be a boy or a girl? And then I felt sick from thinking of the inevitable encounter. "Are you okay? Should I pull over or something? I mean we're almost there..."

I gulped and waved a hand at her. "No. I'm fine. The sick feeling comes and goes." Luz let go a breath she seemed to be holding, relieved. Looking out the window, I noticed that Luz hadn't been lying. Queens Heights stood a good few feet from us, and when Luz pulled into a parking lot we got out. She took my hand and asked anxiously, "Are you ready?" I smiled despite all else because I knew she'd been looking forward to the one-on-one time with Joey. I squeezed her hand gently and whispered, "As ready as I'll ever be, Luz."

When we entered I could feel all eyes on us—well, me. The lights were dimmed and there were tons of kids in the large auditorium. Even though the radio was blaring, "E.T." by Katy Perry, I could still hear what people were saying. *"Oh, my gosh, is that Reina Reyes?" "Yeah, I*

heard about her kid, too." "Isn't she the one dating Emilio?"
"Yeah, I hear she made him drop out of school, again."

I closed my eyes and kept forward, unwilling to allow their insults to get to me. I turned to Luz and she smiled at me warmly. Yes, I was here for Luz. I just had to keep reminding myself that. If I did that then I'd bear through the night. Luz spotted Joey and started toward him. She stopped and turned to face me. "Oh, I could stay with you if—"

"Go ahead and have fun. I'll just go over and get myself some punch." She hesitated. I smiled a smile I didn't feel and nudged her in Joey's direction. "Joey's waiting for someone to dance with. Go ahead." Luz giggled, thanked and hugged me and flitted over to her boyfriend as happy as ever. I sighed and went over to the empty tables and sat. I hadn't even bothered with the punch; instead I just sat there, and watched as people danced. Song after song.

And that's when I saw *him.*

With a swagger of his own, Emilio entered the auditorium with a petite black girl at his side. Her hair was flaming red—as was her outfit. Studying closely, it looked as if there were fake horns on her head. I recognized that familiar snobby air immediately as Robyn Newton. Emilio was smiling brightly and looking as sexy as ever. Compared to the last time I saw him, he looked like a god. His hair was gelled back, his teeth bright, and beard gone. His tuxedo even looked spiffy and brand new. Robyn clung to him as if he were her lifeline. Where he moved she moved. I wanted to look away, but I couldn't. And it wasn't as if it were due to his sex appeal, like why everyone else was ogling him, but just because I missed him. My Emilio...

He whispered something in Robyn's ear and kissed her on the cheek at the sight of her disappointment. I rolled my eyes and finally turned my head. I couldn't stand to watch that any longer. The radio was playing a slow song by Jon B., called, "They Don't Know." When a sudden deep voice snatched me from my daydreaming I flinched. "Care for this dance, my lady?" I looked up to see Emilio smiling down at me, his hand extended out to me. Gazing deep in his eyes my heart betrayed me instead, "Of course." He helped me up and led me to the middle of the dance floor. It was as if I were at home twirling and holding him close to me. Like all the bad things never happened—or weren't as bad—when he held me. My eyes were closed and my head rested on his chest when he whispered, "I miss you, Ray."

I smiled at the words I waited so long to hear. "Me, too." He laughed and held me tighter. And then, all too soon, the song ended. Everyone was talking loudly when I asked, "Where've you been?" I meant the question to be casual, but I noted the frustration behind them. Emilio turned his head and said simply, "Away." I nodded, deciding not to press him any further. For the moment I wanted to cherish what was going on now. Before I could stop myself, I threw my arms around his waist. When I felt it enough, I began to pull back. Well, when I did that, Emilio leaned down and kissed me fiercely—like he had at the hospital. It undid me. I loved the taste of his lips against mine and how he made me feel. Like I mattered, as if I were the most beautiful thing in the world. I could feel eyes on us and decided to stop. Not really because of that but because of reality instead.

I was pregnant and I deceived Emilio.

That thought alone nearly brought me to my knees in sorrow. Guilt washed through me when I said fearfully, "No. Stop. This isn't right." I put my hands on his chest to stop him but the look he gave me was desperate with need. "What's wrong? You're my girl—what's not right about that?"

I shook my head and whispered, "But Ross..."

He shook his head and said between clenched teeth, "I took care of him." I could feel my heart drop all the way to my toes at those words. He took care of him? Finally, I shoved him away and glared. "What are you talking about?" Emilio was grinning evilly when a shout rang out in the auditorium. I turned to the bloody guy who stumbled inside and recognized him as one of Ross's friends, Tim I thought his name was. "Help!" Tim shouted. The radio that was blaring Borris's, "Monster Mash" instantly stopped. I was the first to meet him as he tumbled to the floor, groaning in pain. "What's wrong? What happened?"

His face was tortured agony when he rasped, "Me and Ross were headed here when a bunch of these guys pull us out of the car." He swallowed and continued. "Just, dear God, somebody go help him. He's dying out there..."

Tim Fainted.

"No!" I was shouting that over and over again as I ran outside into the school parking lot. It was impossible to miss the screaming, broken, guy on the ground. When I reached him, I could feel the school crowd gathering behind me. I was crying so hard that I could barely see his face. There was just so much blood everywhere: his face, arms, legs, stomach, chest—I meant it when I said everywhere. Ross finally stopped shouting when he saw me and began to cry, too. "It hurts to breathe, Queen. I just want the pain to stop..." And then, as I sat there peering down into his eyes I made the same promise he had made me all those weeks ago. "Don't worry." I said. "I'm gonna make the pain go away, Ross. I swear it."

And then everything was happening very quickly: the paramedics came and carefully hauled Ross and Tim into the van and sped off. As they drove away I reached my hand out as if to touch him one more time. Determined now, I wiped the tears from my face and searched the crowd for Luz. I found her in Joey's arms, crying and shaking. My heart broke at the sight of my friend like that and at the promise I broke to her. This was supposed to be a good experience. Shaking away all doubts, I opened my mouth to ask her for her keys when Joey held his hand up to me. He dug around in his pocket for a while and placed a set of keys into my hands. "It's the white *Honda Accord* by the school gates. Go ahead." He said all of that unable to meet my gaze.

Grateful, I nodded my thanks and started for the school gates—eager to reach one of my best friends for at least one last time.

When life gives you oranges...

I FOUND ROSS'S PARENTS and aunt, Spyrit, in the waiting room. *The three of them were huddled* together weeping profoundly. There was a small rush of guilt as I approached them. I didn't want to be intruding on an intimate family moment. And then I remembered Ross standing by my side when my daughter was at her worst. He made a U-turn without question when I told him to go to the hospital. Not complaining about a thing as insignificant as gas money, car trouble, or even time consumption. Even if I was using his time, I sure wasn't wasting it. He chose to be there—by my side.

And there was no way I would turn on him now.

Summoning courage, I prepared to face the music and walked up to them. Spyrit spoke first when she saw me. "So, I see you have given my nephew a chance after all."

I saw how the smile touched her lips and fail to reach her eyes. I nodded, and said through my tears, "Yeah."

"Why *my* baby, Eli?" His mother asked his father brokenly. "He's such a sweet boy—he wouldn't hurt a soul." And then she turned to me and frowned, then realization flecked in her eyes. "Oh, you're the girl I saw with Ross a few weeks back." I wiped the tears that were falling in buckets down my face and extended my hand to her. She shook it while I greeted bleakly, "Reina Reyes, ma'am."

"Cynthia Nolan. And this here is my husband, Eli." I tried to control my wobbly knees but failed and staggered back. Eli helped me to a chair and began to study my face closely. "Sweetie, you look so pale. Have you eaten anything?" I managed to shake my head. He turned to Spyrit and asked, "Could you go and ask one of the nurses to send a plate of food for Reina, Sis?"

Spyrit nodded and went to the circulation desk.

I was suffering. If Ross died, I didn't know how I could survive from the stress. Closing my eyes, I tried to think of something to alleviate the pain. The first time I met Ross, how he knew how to press my buttons, his smile, his laugh, his teasing, the way he looked at me, the love he felt for me even when I didn't return it, how he held me, that afternoon we spent together making love, the child he gave me. I smiled at that, even though it defied logic and how much I, admittedly, had doubts about keeping this baby—at that moment I realized I couldn't. I wouldn't. I couldn't picture killing my little round-shaped face son or daughter; of never being allowed to meet that little person Ross and I created.

"Pretty dress." A squeaky voice said to me. I opened my eyes to see a little girl watching me with innocent curiosity. Cynthia and Eli were talking to each other on the other side of the room. "Are you 'bout to get married, Miss?" The little black girl couldn't have been over three or four tugging on the fluffiness of my dress. I smiled through my tears and forced the best smile I could. "No. This is my Halloween costume."

"Oh!" Her face brightened at the mention of Halloween. "I love Halloween!" Her face fell suddenly.

I frowned and asked, "What is it?" She glanced around uneasily. "I can't go trick-or-treating this year 'cause mommy's sick. I was here all day with my aunt Marie—" She pointed to the circulation desk where a heavyset woman maybe in her late thirties was filling out paper-work. At the mention of her name, she turned around to glare at me suspiciously. "Kelly, come over here girl! It's time to go home now." She skipped over to the cantankerous woman and turned back to smile at me before they both left. *Well, that was interesting*, I thought. Even though my heart ached for Kelly, I had demons of my own to deal with. And when the doctor came from around the corner he stopped before the Nolan's and smiled a smile that didn't look very inviting. He looked sad, grim almost. I stood and staggered over to where they stood. The doctor regarded me with a tight smile too, and that's when I knew something was wrong. I could feel it. I placed a hand over my heart as if to shield it from the inevitable agony that would soon come crashing over me. "I'm Doctor Ellis. And I assume you two are the patient's parents?" Whereas my family would have lashed out at the simple question, the Nolan's kept their cool. "Yes, doctor. Is our son all right?" Eli said hopefully, but I heard the doubt laced with it. Dr. Ellis grounded his teeth together before he said, "Well, from our observation, we saw that Ross suffered a severe spinal injury. Whoever did this to him, they knew what they were doing and how to hurt him."

Cynthia shook her head vigorously and asked, sobbing, "What are you saying Dr. Ellis?"

At the doctor's next words I wanted to faint. "Well, there's an eighty-eight percent chance that your son will never walk again. I'm so sorry."

It was then when I realized how very wrong I had been. When the sun comes out light doesn't always touch everything, because there will always be dark places that can become a haven of grief. Misery. Terror. Pain.

It is people's choices that determine if light will contact them at all.

In other words, in order for light to truly touch everything of you—then you must step into it.

Epilogue

ROSS

ROSS WOKE UP TO the sound of crying. Of course, he knew who that was. Sitting up, he grabbed his cane and walked rigidly over to his son's, Ross Junior, crib. Ever since the accident at that Halloween Dance a year ago, where he had gotten jumped by those gangbangers, it had left him unable to walk for a solid four months. The medics deemed it impossible for him to ever walk again, but with a little determination and rehab—he was able to defy all logic. Even though his movements were still a little stiff at times, hence the cane. So now he was to begin his senior year of high school, unable to try out for any sports, running hurt his back.

Sitting his cane aside, he moved around a little to work the kinks from his back. When that was accomplished, he leaned over to lift his son agilely in his muscled arms. Oh yeah, rehabilitation meant lots of upper body strength. His leg muscles were beginning to function normally, but it still felt uncomfortable at times. Through all of it—the pain, struggle, depletion, worthlessness—he couldn't have moved on if it wasn't for his family supporting him the entire way. His mother, Cynthia, staying with him through the nights the cramps in his back were the worst. His father, Eli, working extra hard to find a replacement Waiter in the café and go over important business where it was concerned in New York. His aunt, Spyrit, making a habit to travel between Philadelphia and New York just to make sure he was okay. And then there was Reina...

Reina Reyes had given him everything; a life, a beautiful baby boy, and nearly a year of showing him how to love again. Every day after school since he'd been injured, she'd stop by; bring RJ, and a bunch of notes. The school had told him that he'd have to repeat his senior year, but Ross didn't mind. It was better actually; it meant that he could graduate with Reina. And anywhere she was was where he wanted to be.

"Ooooh!" RJ babbled as Ross began to pat his back, hoping he'd return to sleep. Ross yawned and looked over at the digital clock that told him it was ten in the morning—Reina would be coming over soon. She often visited early on the weekends to deliver RJ to him or to pick him up. Ross never understood why she was such a morning bird, but it was something he wouldn't change about her. Ross cradled his son all the way toward his king-sized bed and dressed him mildly for the warm August weather. RJ was quiet now and that thought alone had Ross speeding to RJ's crib.

Until his cell phone rang.

RJ began to fuss louder than the ringtone. Juggling his son in one arm, he snatched the black iPhone from his desktop and pressed the talk button. "Hello?" He asked gruffly from deprivation of sleep. RJ was still crying and reaching out for the phone Ross spoke into.

"Is that *my* baby crying? Uh-uh, let me in Ross." Reina warned from the other line. Ross lived just above the café, having an entire apartment to himself while his parents lived just down the street in a typical upper-middle-class suburban home. Ross convinced his parents that he was old enough for his own apartment before the accident. Even though they were skeptic at the idea of leaving him on his own, they upheld their end of the deal. He gave all of his family members a key to the café and apartment, just in case. Which included Reina...

"Why don't you have your key, missy?" Ross asked teasingly as he descended the stairs leading to the stream. He saw Reina outside in a yellow sundress. Her hair was also cropped short into a bob of light brown curls. She also wore a sparkling headband, the one he bought for her a short time ago, and was carrying a giggling two-year old in her arms. Jasmine Reyes was Reina's first born daughter who Ross absolutely adored. Even though she wasn't his, he loved her just as much as he did RJ. Ross hung up the phone, dug out his keys from his jammies and unlocked the door. Reina was smiling brightly when she answered, "Enrique came over crying like a baby all night and keeping me awake about how scared he was of the great Angela-zilla. She was having cravings and Ricky didn't know what to do, where to go and why—so all night we went on a wild goose-hunt for chocolate turtles." She shook her head and sat Jasmine at one of the rounded tables. Ross chuckled, "I don't blame the man. You were scary enough when you were pregnant with RJ." Glaring, Reina happily took RJ from Ross and he let out a sigh of relief. Ross was always worried of dropping his son when he walked anywhere with him. Reina looked down and cooed to their three-month old, "You're mommy's beautiful little man, aren't you? Gonna grow up to be nice and strong like your daddy, huh?" Reina looked up to catch Ross wincing. Damn, he really hated it when she made that face. That, *"Oh no, you should really go lie down"* face. Rolling his eyes he reached a hand out to tousle her light brown curls. "I'm fine, Queen. Just relax." Ross walked stiffly to the coffee machines and called over his shoulder, "Up for some coffee, *chica?*"

"Sure." She answered, though Ross could still hint the worry in her voice. Ross sighed and turned fully around. "Look at me, Reina." She reluctantly met his gaze and shifted her son in her arms. Ross scratched his shoulder length dreads and trudged over to where his love stood before him. After kissing her forehead, he pulled her into his arms, careful not to smother RJ though. When Reina looked up, her large brown eyes were glassy. "I just worry about you sometimes, Ross. Ever since that Halloween dance—"

Ross bent to kiss Reina on the lips to silence her—and keep her from crying. When he pulled back, her face was rose red and her eyes were still closed as if she were savoring it. When she finally opened her eyes, he smiled and whispered, "It's all over now. That was the past." Reina looked doubtful at first but then she stood on her toes to give him one last peck on his lips. "You're right, and besides, we have more important matters to discuss."

Ross nodded, "Right."

"Like who's putting the baby back to sleep."

"Right." Ross repeated dutifully.

"And who's making the coffee." She listed.

He nodded again. "Yep."

"And if we want a spring wedding or an autumn one." She said suggestively.

Ross nodded, not really paying attention. "Uh-huh." When he realized what she was saying he widened his eyes and stuttered, "Y-You're asking me t-to—"

"I do." Reina said finally, stood on her toes, and placed a smoldering kiss on Ross's lips.

Jasmine giggled.

Song for Ross and Reina: "Daydreamer" by Adele

EMILIO

Prison. It wasn't as hyped up as people made it seem in the movies. There was no black and white striped uniform and the little cell that sat next to the bailiff's desk.

It was far worse.

There was no daylight here unless they were outside pulverizing the bricks with axes. The only alone time he ever got was with...hell, no one. But, there was a silver lining in it all though; he still had his poetry.

Sitting up in his bunk, he grunted and reached under his pillowcase to retrieve his latest piece. Emilio closed his eyes and savored every word he'd read over a thousand times.

My beauty, my star

I'll always love you

Just the way you are

I'll never forget

The first time we met

Losing you was a sad loss—

To that bastard Ross...

At the mention of that bitch's name made Emilio tremble with hate. Hell, he never knew he could loathe a person so profoundly until he fought that asshole. Losing Reina was like losing his life. And the fact that she spoke against him in court changed a lot of things. For one, he was gone for good now because it was his third offense. Also, his gang promised him that if he ever made it out someday, that they'd be all over him. And, finally, her doing that to him made him kind of...resent her.

Hate her.

Anger roiled through him at all he sacrificed to show Reina how much he still loved her, how much he missed her. He had been so close to having her in his bed that night at the dance, *his* bed, that he could've tasted it. Ever since her first born, he found it hard to ever even trust her again. So much so, that he found himself doing it anyway—trusting her. Emilio scoffed at that, doing just that got him where? In the can. And her— pregnant again. Why the hell had he even tried to love the whore again? Like things would've ever changed. Emilio shrugged. *Well,* he thought, *if I wasn't in here for trying to kill that Rasta bastard Reina would have probably served as a close second.*

Smiling at the thought of it, Emilio "borrowed" one of his cellmate's pencils and began to jot it down.

Song for Emilio: "Make You Mine" by 2AM Club

ENRIQUE

"Ricky! Hurry up with dinner—I'm starving!" Enrique nearly fell as he hurried into the living room to hand over Angela's, his wife, plate. She took it and frowned at the sight of it. "What is this?"

Wiping his sweat-drenched face, he said tiredly, "It's a burrito, baby."

Her eyes widened innocently. "Oh." She hesitantly took a bite and grinned delightedly. "It tastes *good.*"

Enrique chuckled and leaned down to kiss his cranky wife on the cheek. All freaking day he had been in the kitchen for her, making whatever it was she craved. It wasn't like he was complaining or anything, he loved her with all his heart, but damn. It was one of his only days off from work and he'd been dirt-tired.

Most of his co-workers often teased him for being so tight with his time.

"Looks like ol' Ricardo here has had enough for today, huh?" Dan, a close friend of his, said as they clocked out for the day.

"Yeah," Jackson, another co-worker, agreed playfully. "It seems our boy here is *whipped.*" And with that, the forty-year old began to make spanking gestures with his hands.

Enrique laughed. "Oh shut the hell up you pansies." He continued and started for his car. "*Y'all* just mad 'cause *y'all* ain't got a woman as fine as mine."

"You're right." Jackson agreed, wheezing with laughter. "Mines so old her breast milk turned powdered now!"

"Nah!" Dan waved his statement away. "Mines so old her social security number is five!"

Enrique laughed and finally called goodbye to his elder coworkers before he drove on home.

"Ricky!" Angela whined.

Enrique shook his head and sighed, "What now, girl?"

"Could ya?" She frowned and pointed to her slipper-ed feet with a manicured nail. He narrowed his eyes suspiciously at her before he complied. Sitting at the end of the sofa, he began to massage her feet.

"Oh!" She exclaimed.

Enrique smiled to himself; he was finally doing something right today. Out of nowhere, she leaned down and swatted his hands away.

"Hey!" He said, offended.

"I said 'ow' Ricky. That usually means to stop." Sighing, she shoved her empty plate in his hands, yawned and stretched out to sleep.

"Three months pregnant and you're already turning into a zilla." He grumbled as he stomped off toward the sink. He rinsed her plate and placed it in the dishwasher. Rubbing his eyes, he sauntered off into the living room and stared down at his wife. She was breathing evenly now which signaled that she was asleep. She looked so vulnerable lying there like that, so open. He could do anything he wanted with her while in that state—and yet she trusted him. That thought alone made him want to do back flips into the night. But it was times like this where he often missed his family. He could just picture what they were all doing now: His father, Pablo, was probably watching a game or handling some bills. His mother, Gabriella, would now be avidly reading through an English dictionary studying words to learn.

And then there was Reina.

He smiled at the thought of his little sister. She just had her son, RJ, and was better than ever. Last he heard she had a job in a café and was proposing to her son's father. Yeah, as strange as it sounded he could still remember the day she called him up and asked him for advice on how to propose.

"So I just get on one knee and ask him?" She inquired.

Ricky chuckled at the image and replied, "You know *he's* supposed to ask *you,* right?"

Reina scoffed over the phone and said, "I know, I know, but it's like he wants to ask me but never does. I'm just so sick and tired of waiting. I mean, I'll say yes if he asks." He shook his head at the love in her voice. Hmm. Enrique thought over it and decided that Ross was a cool guy. He was a good step up from Juan, and an awesome step up from Emilio.

Emilio. Last he heard from his "friends" back in Queens, he was locked up from assaulting Ross Nolan. The psycho had left the guy almost completely unable to walk, and was shit now in Enrique's book. Huh, he just had the *best* choice in friends.

Sighing, Enrique carried Angela all the way into the room and laid her on the bed. She was shivering from the air conditioner, so he tucked her in tightly and gave her a quick kiss on the lips before he started for the door.

"I love you, Ricky..." Angela whispered almost unintelligibly from sleep.

Enrique smiled at the words that lifted his heart and whispered, "I love you, too, baby," before he turned the light out and closed the door behind him. *Now*, he thought to himself, *time to clean that kitchen...*

Song for Enrique and Angela: "Fool For You" by Cee-lo Green

JUAN

"Why is it so hot?" Naomi Jacobs whined. Actually, she complained all the way to their, Juan's and hers, two o' clock class. Juan chuckled at the unexpected outburst. That was Naomi for you. Juan smiled good-naturedly and pulled her against him suddenly. Her whines immediately stopped then. "What's this about? Am I complaining too much for you?"

Juan pulled back a little. "No."

She narrowed her eyes, "Uh-huh. Every time I start to *speak my mind* you just up and hug me out of the blue." She said and pulled fully back from his arms to glare up at him. The halls were thinning now, so they had enough privacy to talk in confidence. Juan flashed an all-star grin and leaned down to meet her eyes. "That's not true babe—I'm just trying to seduce you."

Naomi looked away, totally flushed.

Juan sighed and said, "Well, I see that's working wonders." He and Naomi were just study buddies, but they both made a point to see each other for reasons other than studying. It was a completely platonic relationship; he knew stuff about her past like why she came to college on scholarship because her family had barely a penny to their name. In hearing that, he felt for the girl. Of all the lavish things he'd wasted throughout his life, he'd never once even begin to appreciate things more than Naomi. She also knew about his past, or reality, too. Like Jasmine and how much he loved her and saw her only on every other weekend. The visitation wasn't much, but he still got to have her during the holidays—so it was a win-win situation. She also knew about Reina and what terms they were on. They spoke only if it was where their daughter was concerned. Like the time she'd been hospitalized for a week because of the pneumonia she developed. Thinking of that day—that hopeless afternoon—made him want to hit things even more. He was in class when his cell vibrated to reveal a sobbing Mrs. Reyes—Reina's mom. "Juan, oh my gosh—Yaz is in the hospital." It took a moment for it to really sink in because of the paper he was working on. "Wait, what?" He nearly screeched, drawing so much attention it nearly got him kicked out of class. Juan stood instantly and dashed out the door—cursing Reina the entire drive. How could she let that happen? Oh yeah, *her* life was so flawed. *Her* issues were all that mattered. *Her* problems were all anyone should stress over. But Jasmine? Juan scoffed; it was only a wonder why Reina hadn't polluted their daughter into hating him yet. Shit, if only he wasn't in school—he would have sued the hell out her for Jasmine. When Juan had thoughts like that it made him have to remember that it was over. That Jasmine was full and healthy and that he had to visit her sometime this weekend. He was due to.

"Juan? Are you sad?" This was one of the many reasons he loved his Mimi. Through all the two years they'd known each other her innocence was what kept his hands to himself. She'd told him that she was a virgin, and Juan would be damned if he ever destroyed something so valuable to his Mimi. Never again was he stealing *anyone's* virtue.

Juan wrapped an arm loosely around Naomi's shoulder and ruffled her angelic blond hair. "Nah, I'm just thinking about Jasmine. It's about time I visit her soon." Juan smiled at the thought of seeing her again. "God, how I miss that girl."

"Oh." Her blue eyes scorched him.

Juan leaned down to place a kiss on her forehead. "There's more to it than that isn't it? I know you Mimi."

When she looked up her eyes were sad. "I just thought that you were getting annoyed with me. I don't like it when you tap your feet." Yes, Juan tapped his feet to an inaudible tune when he was overwhelmed. Just the fact that she knew everything about him made him smile. "No, I could never be mad at you, angel." She laughed and he teased, "Besides, you know I *love* you."

Naomi laughed at that and said, "Oh, I love you too Juan. But you scare me sometimes." They began to saunter off a little ways down the hall. Naomi sighed and leaned against the wall—looking up into Juan's eyes. Watching her like that, so genuine and innocent looking made him want her with a need so bad he could barely stand it. Juan placed an arm against the wall above her and leaned down, his lips brushing hers. Naomi's eyes were fluttering when she said nervously, "W-What are—"

Juan placed a finger to her lips and challenged, "You said you loved me right?" His aura was filled with desire and dark humor. It was when Juan's voice got all husky that way made Naomi want to swoon. She nodded slightly. Shyly. Juan pecked her lips once and said, "Prove it then." Juan leaned down to meet her lips and suddenly there were fireworks. It was *nothing* like this with Reina. Maybe it was because he was drunk that night, maybe it wasn't, but it still couldn't compare to this. Where their drunken encounter was quick and sloppy, his and Naomi's was slow and sensual. Naomi began to unbutton his shirt and grind up against him when, Lord help him, Juan held back. Re-buttoning his shirt he nipped her bottom lip and said lowly, "Uh-uh. This isn't the time or place for this angel." God, he was so not sated right now he could curse. But no, he wouldn't do that to his Mimi, not ever.

Or, at least, not yet.

"So, I'm not good enough?" She said, straightening, blushing, and keeping her gaze to the ground. "I bet Reina was way prettier than me anyway. What was I thinking?"

He knew she meant the words to herself, but as she turned to walk back to class, he grabbed her by the arm and pulled her into his arms. "Never that, angel—never that."

"All right." She sighed in relief before standing on her toes and delivered one final kiss to him. "Then let us see what Professor Irv's class awaits for us. Shall we?"

Juan chuckled, kissed her on the forehead, and took her hand to begin walking down the hall and a path to a great future with Naomi. "We shall, angel. We shall."

Song for Juan: "Right Where You Want Me" by Jesse McCartney

About the author

SINCE THE AGE OF twelve, Laura could always be found writing. She writes within a wide array of genres, including paranormal, drama, slice of life, and (her favorite) romance. In her free time, if she's not writing, she's reading or listening to a steamy audio-book. Her most notable works include Something About Kyle and her ongoing, The REAL Series, which explores the narratives of various, interconnected young adults.

As an author, Laura aims to push boundaries and leave a lasting impact on her community. Her journey taught her the importance of perseverance, creativity, and staying true to one's unique vision. Support her craft by purchasing from her bookstore.

Other books in this series:

GRAY- 1

LIGHT- 2

CAVE - 3

*EDGE - 4

HEART - 5

SECRETS - 6

HOME -7

SHAME - 8

*written by *Laurie Ross*